THE SCRABBLEMONGERS

MARGOT BOSONNET started writing when her children grew up. She is the author of *Skyscraper Ted and Other Zany Verse; Up the Red Belly; Red Belly, Yellow Belly; and Beyond the Red Belly* (all published by Wolfhound Press). She works in Trinity College Library.

The Scrabblemongers

Margot Bosonnet

WOLFHOUND PRESS

Published in 2001 by
Wolfhound Press Ltd
68 Mountjoy Square
Dublin 1, Ireland
Tel: (353-1) 874 0354
Fax: (353-1) 872 0207

© 2001 Margot Bosonnet

All rights reserved. No part of this book may be reproduced or utilised in any form or by any means digital, electronic or mechanical including photography, filming, video recording, photocopying, or by any information storage and retrieval system or shall not, by way of trade or otherwise, be lent, resold or otherwise circulated in any form of binding or cover other than that in which it is published without prior permission in writing from the publisher.

This book is fiction. All characters, incidents and names have no connection with any persons living or dead. Any apparent resemblance is purely coincidental.

 The Arts Council / An Chomhairle Ealaíon   Wolfhound Press receives financial assistance from The Arts Council/ An Chomhairle Ealaíon, Dublin, Ireland.

British Library Cataloguing in Publication Data
A catalogue record for this book is available from the British Library.

ISBN 0-86327-880-9

5 4 3 2 1

Cover Image: Aileen Caffrey
Typesetting and book design: Wolfhound Press
Printed in the UK by Cox & Wyman Ltd, Reading Berks.

To all those workers

who deal with the leftovers of our lives

– 1 –

The Scrabblemongers

At the bottom of a winding country road, six miles from the nearest town, lived a family called the Scrabblemongers.

Bobby was the eldest. Then came Primrose, who was just a little bit younger. Finally there was baby Starlight, who hadn't yet learned how to walk ...

... And, of course, their mother and father, Mr and Mrs Scrabblemonger. Mr and Mrs Scrabblemonger didn't refer to each other as 'Mr' and 'Mrs' — Mr Scrabblemonger called his wife Emerald, and Mrs Scrabblemonger called her husband Pandy.

They were quite poor. Pandy had been out of work for a long time. Once he had been employed in a big mill, but the mill had closed down and he was unable to find another job. So he had to take what he could get — a bit here, a bit there. People called him the odd-job man. But sometimes the jobs were very odd indeed, and not too frequent, and not very well paid either, so money was scarce.

The only reason they even had a house was because of the dump.

They lived in a nice little stone cottage that Pandy had bought very cheaply before his payoff money from the mill ran out. The reason it was so cheap was because of its position right beside the County Council dump. All day long, bin-lorries and tipper lorries and cars and trailers and trucks rumbled by, piled with loads of refuse of every description — and nobody else wanted to live beside a rubbish dump.

The Scrabblemongers didn't particularly want to, either. However, when it's a choice between living beside a rubbish dump and having nowhere to live at all ... well, that's a different story — and the house itself was fine. The dump was on the site of an old quarry, and the house had been built before the land even became a quarry. The quarry-owner had lived there. So it was a sturdy house, able to stand up to the vibrations of machinery and the blasting of rocks. The comings and goings of a tip-head were nothing by comparison.

People called the Scrabblemongers odd for living in such a place. But the Scrabblemongers weren't odd. They were a perfectly ordinary family forced by circumstances to live beside a dump. So they did what everyone has to do at times — they made the best of things. In fact, that was the family motto. Pandy had embroidered the words in coloured threads on a piece of old flour-sack and hung it in the kitchen from a bamboo stick. It made a beautiful wall-hanging, and it was entirely washable as well.

It was important that things be washable in the Scrabblemonger household, for they had a problem with dust. This didn't come from the dump itself, where they had a hose spraying the wheels of cars in dry weather and a big trough of water for lorries to drive through to keep the dust down; but the road outside their front gate was powdery white from the comings and goings of so many dirty vehicles.

The dust blew over the Scrabblemongers' house and settled like ash on the back lawn. Pandy and Emerald were forever scrubbing and cleaning. Bobby and Primrose and baby Starlight all had to be bathed at least twice a day — once in the morning, and once in the evening, and sometimes once in the middle of the day as well. But they didn't mind. They had always been used to this, and they thought everyone else did the same.

The Scrabblemongers' back garden was very long, surrounded by a thick hedge with a sturdy chain-link fence behind it. The whole garden was planted with grass. The dusty state of this didn't bother Primrose and Bobby; they had their Tree-house, and that was where they spent most of their time. Pandy had built it in the fork of a big tree at the bottom of the garden. It was a bony old tree with few leaves, even in summer. Emerald said it was just as well it was good for something.

The Tree-house had a red-tiled roof, three proper glass windows that opened and closed, and a little veranda by the front door where they could sit with their legs dangling down. There was a rope ladder to get up to it, and a marvellous slide down from one side in case they needed to get away in a hurry. Pandy had made this from a plank of wood, which he had sanded and varnished and polished to a high shine; and if it became dusty, well, that only made it all the slippier for sliding.

Primrose and Bobby met other children at school, but nobody came to play with them at home. They were never invited to other people's houses, either. So in the holidays, especially the summer holidays, they didn't see any other children for weeks on end. Still, they had each other, and they were lucky in that.

They had a dog, too — though it wasn't a real one. Emerald said that wouldn't be fair. The garden was too dusty, and anyway, she couldn't be washing a dog three times a day. So they had a pretend dog instead.

Pandy had found a perfectly good kennel in the dump one day. He painted it red and put it in one corner of the garden, beneath the dining-room window. It made the garden look cosy, and it was good for security, Pandy said.

They called their pretend dog Shadow. He was jet-black, and he followed after them or ran before them, depending on where their shadows were, for he always kept in the shade. When he wasn't in his kennel, or playing with them, he snoozed under the slide, where he lay guarding the Tree-house.

So everyone in the family made the best of what they had. The funny thing was that Bobby and Primrose thought nobody, *nobody*, was as lucky as they were, because of their Tree-house, and because of all the wonderful things that went on in the dump, right there at the bottom of the garden.

– 2 –

The Tree-house

'Shh!' whispered Primrose. 'Here they come!'

She was sitting outside the Tree-house with Bobby, enjoying the sunshine. Above, a single crow circled the tree, eyeing the slices of bread-and-butter they'd hung from the branches.

Out on the dump, the rest of the crows rose up in a cloud to join it. They circled warily, flew back out over the dump, then wheeled around to circle the tree again. They did this several times, until the bravest crow alighted on one of the topmost branches. In twos and threes the others followed, until there was a black canopy of crows overhead, cawing and shifting and flapping their wings as they eyed the food. The fact that they never managed to fly down and steal the slices didn't stop them sitting there in hope.

Primrose and Bobby surveyed the crows with glee — for now they themselves were famous magicians, and all the birds were their mortal enemies, whom they had turned into crows. The crows had come to plead and beg to be turned back into humans again.

'What about that one?' Primrose whispered, watching a huge crow stretch its wings.

'Old Beakface? No way!' Bobby hissed. 'He's staying like that. Gave us a lot of bother in his day, he did. Serves him right!'

'Well, the quiet one, then? I feel a bit sorry for him.' Primrose nodded at a bird over to the left, which was watching them sadly.

'OK. He's been punished enough. We can let him go.'

Primrose grinned, and together they began to chant quietly:

'Bubble, bubble,
On the double,
Begone! and cause us
No more trouble!'

At the word *'Begone!'* they both stood up and shouted, waving their arms in the air. All the crows took fright and flew off in a panic, out over the dump, where they milled around in great confusion for a while, before the slices of bread-and-butter tempted them back to their high perches in the tree. Bobby and Primrose never got tired of this game, and nor did the crows.

14

Emerald had come out into the garden to hang some washing on the line.

'Leave those poor demented birds alone!' she called, making the crows fly up in a panic once again. She knew that Bobby and Primrose could tease them all day.

'They like it,' Primrose yelled. 'It's fun. They get bored just flying around.'

Bobby slid quickly down the slide and ran up the garden to Emerald.

'Has Pandy finished our telescope yet?'

'Pandy's gone for a walk with Starlight.'

'But he promised!'

'Give the man a chance,' laughed Emerald. 'Hasn't he been at it for weeks?'

'But he said it would be finished today.'

'And so it will, Mr Impatience. It just needs a final polish.'

'We don't care if it's not polished. We just want to use it.'

'Well, Pandy cares. You know how particular he is.'

Bobby sighed.

Pandy had found the telescope weeks ago. It was a huge, heavy, brass one, and when he first saw it, it was encrusted with cement-like dirt. But he recognised how good it was and set to work restoring it to its former glory.

It was an old ship's telescope, Pandy said. He was going to mount it on a stand by the back window of the Tree-house, so they could see everything for miles around. But the cleaning and polishing process seemed to go on forever, and Bobby was seething to use it.

Pandy, however, was firm about not cutting corners. 'You'll get it when it's ready, not before.' But he had promised it to them today.

Bobby went back to the Tree-house, disappointed.

'You're too impatient,' said Primrose. 'It's only morning still. If Pandy said it'll be finished today, then it'll be finished today.'

'When we're in bed, probably,' Bobby grumbled.

Primrose laughed at the truculent look on his face and said, 'Let's get the bread down and go look out the window.'

They retrieved the slices of bread-and-butter and took them into the Tree-house to play with again later on, or to eat in the afternoon when they might be peckish. Primrose stood by the doorway, surveying their den with quiet satisfaction.

'It's a brilliant Tree-house, isn't it?'

The Tree-house was as solid as a rock. Pandy had made it out of thick planks of timber that he had rescued from the dump. And instead of building it completely in the fork of the tree, he had allowed a couple of branches to come inside and be part of the Tree-house itself. So they had a branch going through one corner near the roof, and another branch running up by the window that looked out towards the house and Shadow's kennel. But the middle was totally clear, and that made quite a big space.

Underneath two of the windows they had long chests with lift-up lids, for storing things in. The chests could be used as beds, for the lids were padded and covered with flowery material that matched the curtains.

'It's the best Tree-house in the world,' said Bobby, 'and it'll be even better when we get our telescope.'

He opened the back window, which faced the dump, and the two of them looked out over their familiar landscape.

For as far as they could see, there were acres and acres of filled-in land, covered with weeds. Much of the land was divided into big square sections by high wire-netting fences nailed to timber poles. In windy weather the fences were festooned with sheets of newspaper and plastic bags, rising and falling with each gust of wind, or blowing up to flap frantically against the wire.

'Look at the giant birds!' Bobby always said.

'No, they're ghosts!' Primrose would declare dramatically. 'Caged ghosts, trapped by daylight — helpless with their night-time powers gone....'

Every so often a council worker would go around collecting up the loose papers, and they'd have to wait for their birds and ghosts to reappear.

There was no wind today. Primrose and Bobby hung out the window and stared down into their moat.

'There aren't many people who have moats around their houses,' said Bobby proudly.

'Only people in castles.'

17

'And us. Too bad it's not full of water.'

'Then we wouldn't be able to see the Sandwich!' Primrose protested with a wail. The Sandwich was just as important as the moat.

Bobby looked sheepish. 'I forgot.'

The dump surrounded the Scrabblemongers' garden on three sides, but it didn't come right up to the fence. So what Bobby and Primrose saw when they looked down from their Tree-house was a wall of rubbish all around, separated from their garden by a very deep, wide trench with stony soil on the bottom. This was their moat.

The wall of rubbish formed a giant sandwich, layered with all sorts of interesting things. Sometimes Primrose and Bobby got down out of the tree and squeezed in behind the hedge, where they could stand up against the chain-link fence and view it even better.

There were black bin-bags hanging out, some in tatters, some with interesting bulges. Arms of woolly jumpers hung down here and there; bits of carpet stuck out; and they could see planks, pipes, mattresses, machinery, boxes, car tyres, metal drums, and bits of brightly coloured plastic. There was even a wheelbarrow bedded in at one point. Another place had a sofa wedged in a pile of rubble. Close by was a large suitcase. You could study the Sandwich for weeks and not notice everything there was to see.

'Wouldn't it be great if we could get down into the moat?' Bobby stared longingly at all these things just out of reach.

'Pandy would kill us!'

It was strictly forbidden. They had been well warned — and, anyway, Pandy made sure the chain-link fence was kept in good order, with no holes for adventurous children to slip through. So that was that.

'Dinner!'

Emerald was standing by the clothesline, calling. Bobby and Primrose shut the window, tumbled down the slide and raced each other up the garden to the back door.

– 3 –

Emerald

Emerald had made a nice shepherd's pie — their favourite. She dished it up while Pandy fed Starlight, who was sitting in her high chair. Starlight might not be able to walk, but she could sure polish off a plateful of shepherd's pie.

'Mmmma ... ma ... ma,' she said between mouthfuls, making Emerald smile.

Emerald was a very special person — apart from the fact, of course, that she was the mother of Primrose and Bobby and baby Starlight.

To look at, she seemed like any other mother who worked in the home — always busy about the house, washing, ironing, mending, minding the baby, shopping, baking buns and pies, or cooking dinners.

But adventure burned inside her like a flame.

Every week she would visit the library in town and come back with armfuls of books on China, Egypt, Tibet,

Mongolia, Morocco, Afghanistan, Antarctica — you name it, and Emerald had read about it. She was a walking encyclopaedia of facts and figures and information about various tribes of people around the world. The books had beautiful photographs and described strange and wonderful places. 'It's the next best thing to being there,' Emerald always said.

And, of course, she couldn't be there, because she had a family to raise and a husband to look after — and, anyway, she had no money to spare for things like that. But she was unshakeable in her belief that sometime, when Bobby and Primrose and Starlight had grown up and gone away to live their own lives, she would travel the world.

'But how will you do all that without money?' Bobby asked.

'I'll walk if needs be, and eat berries, and drink from streams.'

'But you can't walk across oceans!'

'Well,' said Emerald firmly, 'I'll get a job on a ship to pay my passage. I'm going, and that's that! Mind you,' she added, 'if I had the money, I'd buy a Land Rover.' Emerald knew how to drive; she had learnt long before she got married.

'And what about me?' Pandy always pretended to look woebegone.

'You can come too,' said Emerald, 'or you can stay at home and mind the house. Whatever you like — but *I'm* going.'

So, to make up for the fact that it would be many, many years before she could do this, Emerald made plans.

Every winter she plotted a different trip, marking the route out on maps and sending away to embassies and tourist offices for more detailed maps of certain parts of countries she might be passing through. One winter she planned out a trip to Timbuktu, down through the Sahara Desert. Another year it was a trek through the mountains of Nepal. She organised her assaults on mountain ranges with complete thoroughness, researching what passes to use and what time of the year would be best if she wanted to avoid too much snow, or too much rain, or too much heat.

She had certain firm goals that she wanted to achieve, too — to stand in the crater of a volcano, to climb up inside the Great Pyramid of Cheops, to snorkel on a coral reef, and most of all to visit Easter Island, with all its huge stone statues staring out to sea. She had a poster of the Easter Island statues covering one wall of her bedroom. Pandy said it gave him nightmares, but she wouldn't take it down.

And she did more than just read and dream — oh, yes! For Emerald was like all true travellers — practical to the core. She knew she couldn't go wandering around the world without the necessary skills for survival.

So she prepared.

Every day she jogged ten times around the garden before breakfast, to keep fit. This was handy, as Shadow was able to jog along with her and so get his daily dose of exercise.

She got Pandy to teach her carpentry skills, for you never knew when you might need to build a house or a boat. She got a book from the library on sailing for beginners, for there's not much point in building a boat if you don't know how to sail it.

She spent a whole winter learning how to swim — she had never learnt as a child — for you never knew when you might need to swim a river or a lake, or when your boat might overturn. She was very nervous about the swimming classes, so Bobby and Primrose went along with her, to give her courage, and they learnt how to swim too.

Emerald also needed their assistance in other ways.

She had far too many maps to make out on her own, so Primrose and Bobby helped her by colouring in mountain peaks, or naming lakes, or looking at the colour charts beside the maps in their atlases to find out if certain bits of land were mountainous or flat. Emerald had built up a collection of atlases, and what they couldn't find in one, they found in another.

They practised cooking things in a hole in the ground, out in the back garden. This was great fun and always successful. Emerald tried to learn how to make fire by rubbing two sticks together, but somehow she hadn't yet mastered the art. But she had researched what things could safely be eaten raw in an emergency.

'Did you know that, if you were really and truly starving, insects are full of protein?'

'Yuck!' Bobby grimaced; and Primrose said quite definitely, 'I'd rather starve!'

Emerald also studied the stars, for navigation. She found them difficult to remember; so Primrose and Bobby drew her beautiful maps of the sky, with backgrounds of midnight blue, and shiny silver stars glued on in the correct places. They decided to make her a map of the moon and its craters, too. You never knew — she might make it up there someday, and it would be handy to be familiar with the landscape.

So, all in all, helping Emerald with her plans took up a lot of their dark winter evenings. And Emerald said that one day they'd be proud of her — their mother, the Famous Explorer. (Bobby and Primrose thought this a peculiar thing to say; they were proud of her already.)

But until then, she stayed at home and made shepherd's pies; and today she had to cope with Starlight deciding that her half-full dinner-bowl would make a nice hat. Bobby and Primrose laughed as the meat and vegetables slid down Starlight's face and stuck in her hair. Emerald sighed and took her little daughter out of the high chair for yet another bath.

— 4 —

Through the Telescope

'There you are, now!' said Pandy, about mid-afternoon. 'All finished.'

He stood back to look at the beautiful, shiny telescope on its tripod stand. Bobby was hopping around with excitement beside him.

'Can we bring it down to the Tree-house now?' asked Primrose.

'I'll do that for you, lovey; it's a bit heavy for lifting up the ladder.' Pandy folded the stand and clipped the telescope into an upright position. 'Right — away we go!'

Primrose and Bobby raced ahead of him down the garden and swung up the rope ladder to the Tree-house. Pandy made a detour to the garden shed and collected a coil of rope. When he reached the ladder, he uncoiled the rope and tied one end of it firmly around the telescope and its stand; then, carrying the loose end of the rope, he climbed up the ladder to the veranda. Bobby and Primrose watched as Pandy carefully pulled the telescope up after him. Then, while he was untying the rope, they hurried inside to open the back window in readiness. When Pandy came in, he put the stand down beside it. Then he fixed the telescope in a horizontal position, so that it stuck out through the window.

'Let me look first!' Bobby demanded.

Pandy showed them how to swivel the telescope left and right, or up and down, and how to secure it in a vertical position when they wanted to close the window.

Bobby put his eye to the glass. A big bulldozer shot into view, so close that Bobby could see every detail, every nut and bolt. He even recognised the driver.

'It's Mr Boggle!' he shouted in delight.

The bulldozers were Bobby's favourite machinery. They bustled about all day, arranging and rearranging things, spreading soil on top of the rubbish to stop it smelling, and generally keeping the dump clean and tidy — which might seem a very peculiar thing to do. But, in fact, the dump was very tidy — as tidy as a dump could possibly be. It was a bit like housekeeping, really, Emerald said: everything in its place.

Mr Boggle had got his name because of the way Bobby stared whenever Pandy brought him down to the dump to watch the bulldozers at work. 'Don't boggle at me like that!' one driver would yell, every time he went by. So Mr Boggle he became.

Bobby swung the telescope a bit to the right, towards the County Council offices, which were in a small prefabricated building near the main entrance. Mr John, who was in charge of the dump, could usually be found there. The building also contained the mess-room, where Mr Tom, the watchman, and all the other workers at the dump went to have their lunches and tea-breaks.

'I can see Mr Tom. He's really close ... I can even see the smoke from his pipe!' Bobby took his eye away from the glass and looked at Pandy, completely overwhelmed.

'Let me have a try.' Primrose pushed in beside the telescope and swung it around towards the Sandwich. She put her eye to the glass.

'Oh!' She blinked in surprise and stepped back, almost tripping over Bobby, who was just behind her. 'The Sandwich came right up into my face!' she said, bewildered.

Pandy laughed. 'It takes a bit of getting used to. Here, let's have a peep.' He put his eye to the telescope. 'Too near. Look, this is what you have to do.'

He showed them how to adjust the lens so that they could look at things that were far away, or very close up, and still see them clearly.

Primrose tried again, turning the lens-adjuster until she had a sharp picture. The Sandwich was so close now that she could almost reach out and touch it. The suitcase came into view and she held it there for a moment, seeing it properly for the first time. It was brown, with rows of metal studs that glinted in the sunlight. She moved the telescope slowly along the Sandwich, amazed at the way she could see even tiny details.

'Look at the machinery,' said Bobby. 'It's brilliant.'

Primrose turned the telescope around to the far right. A line of bin-lorries headed slowly up the hill towards the tip-head. She adjusted the lens until they came sharply into focus, then moved the telescope ahead to find what she was looking for.

Right at the top of the tip-head, the compactors were at work. Primrose liked these best. They had enormous metal wheels with rows of round bumps on them, which flattened down the rubbish until it was hard and firm. Now they came into focus so clearly that she could see every bump, even at such a distance. It was pure magic!

She turned and gave Pandy a big hug, and Bobby said, 'Thanks, Pandy. Thanks a billion.'

'Once is quite enough! Well, I'll leave you to it. Enjoy yourselves!' Pandy departed, looking pleased.

When he had gone, Bobby and Primrose eyed the telescope, then each other, with the same thought in mind.

Bobby grinned. 'Ship ahoy?'

'Me first,' said Primrose quickly.

'That's not fair!'

'Yes it is.'

'It was my idea.'

'Mine too — and I bagged first.' She ended the argument by grabbing the end of the telescope.

Bobby sat down on one of the chests and waited.

Primrose put an eye to the glass, then moved the telescope slowly along the skyline until an excavator appeared.

'Ship ahoy!' she shouted.

'What kind?'

Primrose thought hard — they had a book about ships and boats in the Tree-house, to help them with this.

'An Arab dhow.'

'How do you know?'

'The funny shape.'

'Where's it coming from?'

Primrose paused for a moment; by the rules of the game, this had to be correct.

'Zanzibar.'

'What's the cargo?'

'Spices.'

'My turn.' Bobby took over the telescope and peered through. A huge tractor, pulling a trailer and a skip, came into sight.

'Ship ahoy!' he yelled.

'What kind?' Primrose demanded.

'Schooner with sails.'

'Where from?'

'Darjeeling.'

Primrose paused, thinking. 'Is Darjeeling a port?'

They got out their big *Reader's Digest* atlas and checked.

'It's not!' Primrose said indignantly, looking at Bobby.

Bobby, who didn't like being wrong, tried to cover up. 'Well, I meant the *cargo* was from Darjeeling.'

'What is it?'

'Tea.'

'OK, then — what port did it sail from?' But Bobby didn't know, and had to consult the atlas again for a suitable port.

They could keep this up for hours. There were so many different kinds of boats, so many countries, so many possible cargoes.

They needed books to help, of course, but they had those — thanks to the day of the Great Book Bonanza. Bobby and Primrose couldn't understand why anybody would want to throw out things like that, but Mr Tom, who was the watchman at the dump, was always saying, 'You'd be surprised! You'd be surprised!' Then he'd shake his head, as if to imply that they didn't know the half of it.

– 5 –

The Great Book Bonanza

Mr Tom was a friend of the family. He often came to the Scrabblemongers' house for a cup of tea, or joined them for a meal when he finished work.

His job was to patrol the dump and to keep un-authorised people away. But he didn't mind Pandy checking to see if anything useful had been left in the public area. Sometimes, indeed, he would send word to the Scrabblemongers if a likely-looking load came in, like nice clean bin-bags with things sticking out through the plastic. He wasn't supposed to do this, of course, but he didn't see why perfectly good items should go to waste if people could still use them.

They had got quite a few bits and pieces this way — such as their lovely pine bookshelves. Pandy had scrubbed and varnished them and given one each to Bobby and Primrose. Baby Starlight didn't need one. She kept her books in a cardboard box, as she always pulled things off shelves anyway.

On the day of the Great Book Bonanza, Mr Tom had come running up to the cottage, calling, 'Pandy! Pandy!' in great excitement.

Pandy had gone off with him immediately, without telling Primrose and Bobby what Mr Tom had found. But a short time later he had come home with four huge heavy-duty sacks full of books. You could see clearly, from the shapes, what they contained. They were very heavy, and Mr Tom had lent Pandy a wheelbarrow to ferry them home.

Mr Tom didn't want any of the books for himself. He lived on his own and was only interested in the sports section of the newspaper, which he read every day. So he didn't mind Pandy taking them all — not one little bit.

When the bags were opened, the Scrabblemongers just stared and stared. It was a treasure trove. There was something for everyone.

Two bags were entirely full of children's books, and the others contained adult stuff. Emerald was ecstatic when she saw the huge pile of *National Geographics*. The *Reader's Digest* atlas had been found here too, and the *Book of Ships* that Bobby and Primrose kept in the Tree-house. There were novels of every description, classics, books of poetry, science fiction, *Reader's Digest*s, thrillers — these were Pandy's favourites.

The children's bag must have contained the entire childhood collection of some boy or girl — they didn't know which, because there were no names on the books, which was strange. There were picture-books for Starlight — even a nice clean rag-book, which Emerald immediately washed anyway. For Primrose and Bobby there were Narnias — *The Lion, the Witch and the Wardrobe* was their favourite, and they'd worn out their own copy. There were also Famous Fives, *The Phoenix and the Carpet*, *Five Children and It*, *The Giltspur* trilogy, *Run with the Wind*, lots of Roald Dahls ... the list went on and on.

'How could anybody throw these out?' asked Primrose, horrified.

Emerald shrugged. 'Somebody's child grew up, I suppose, and they don't need them any more.'

'But they should give them away, not throw them in a dump!'

'Maybe they don't know any children,' Emerald pointed out practically. 'Maybe the child died and they just wanted to get rid of the books quickly.... There must be a reason.'

The books were very clean; they hardly looked used at all, in fact. The Scrabblemongers filled every spare surface in the house with their treasures. It made the place look really cosy, and it meant that none of them ever went short of something good to read.

But the wonderful world of books also made Bobby and Primrose long for adventures of their own — and they were constantly thinking up new ways of making day-to-day life more exciting....

– 6 –

Adventures

'Can we sleep in the Tree-house?' Bobby and Primrose were always asking. But Pandy and Emerald said no — it was too dangerous. They might wake up in the middle of the night and forget where they were and fall out of the tree in the dark. It was out of the question.

But Primrose and Bobby kept begging. They thought it would be marvellous. So Emerald suggested that they could solve the problem by taking an afternoon nap there once in a while.

'We're too old for naps!' Bobby said, disgusted. 'That's for babies!' And Primrose made a face.

'Well, try it,' Emerald insisted. 'It's the summer holidays, and you're always up at cockcrow — I don't know how you keep going at all. A nice sleep in the afternoon wouldn't do you one bit of harm. You could pull the curtains in the Tree-house and pretend it's night-time.'

Bobby and Primrose weren't convinced, but Emerald gave them a couple of blankets and two pillows, and the beds looked so inviting that they couldn't wait to try them out.

'You're not to disturb us,' said Primrose. 'You're to let us wake up by ourselves.'

'OK,' laughed Emerald. She had enough to be doing anyway, minding baby Starlight, as Pandy had got a day's work in the town and had gone off on his bicycle very early.

Primrose and Bobby raced down the garden and swung up the rope ladder like a couple of monkeys. They shut the door of the Tree-house after them and pulled the curtains. It made the room look shadowy and mysterious.

Giggling, they climbed onto the beds and pulled the blankets over themselves.

It felt exciting, but they couldn't get to sleep at all. They tried counting sheep, and counting the flowers on the curtains, and pretending their bodies were like clouds floating along in a blue, blue sky. But the more they counted, and the more they pretended, the more awake they became.

Finally, Bobby said crossly, 'This is no use! Let's go and look at the Sandwich.'

They slid down out of the Tree-house and scrambled under the back hedge, where they stared out at the Great Sandwich Mountain, fingers hooked into the chain-link fencing and noses poking through the holes. The crows were picking about among the weeds at the top of the Sandwich. They ignored Primrose and Bobby.

'Look at that,' said Primrose dramatically. 'Even the crows are free ... and here we are, caged up like wild animals, fenced in on all sides!'

She pressed her forehead against the cold wire and looked longingly into the moat.

'I'm going to climb over the fence,' Bobby said with sudden decision. He was annoyed that the sleeping plan had turned out such a flop, and was looking for something new to try. They both stared up at the fence reaching far above their heads.

'Will you be able to get over the top? It's all jagged.'

'I will — just wait and see!'

Bobby tried to get a foothold in the chain-links, but it was nearly impossible. He hooked his fingers through the wire and tried to pull himself up a bit.

'Stand on me.' Primrose knelt down and let Bobby stand on her shoulders. This got him a fairly high grip. There was a supporting cross-wire a third of the way up the fence, and Bobby managed to get his feet onto that and pull himself upwards. He was trying to reach the next supporting wire when he lost his grip and came tumbling heavily down.

He landed on the ground beside Primrose with a thump, and lay winded for a moment. Then he opened his eyes and stared at the chain-link fence in front of him, but didn't get up.

'Are you all right?' Primrose asked anxiously, afraid he had broken a leg or something like that.

Bobby didn't answer; he just reached out and pulled at the wire. Then he sat up and excitedly began to burrow beneath the fencing with his fingers.

'There's a gap here — I can see the bottom of the fence!'

Primrose lay down beside him and looked left and right. The bottom of the wire was buried in the ground for most of the way along, but here it just skimmed the surface.

'We'll hardly squeeze under that!'

'But there's a loose edge — look.' Bobby dislodged a lump of earth with his fingers, and it went rolling down the slope into the bottom of the moat. There was a tiny gap now, and they could see through it clearly.

Primrose knelt beside him and scrabbled at the ground with her fingers, which soon had great wedges of dirt beneath the fingernails. They scraped frantically away at the soil beneath the fence; but once the surface earth was gone they reached harder ground, and their fingers made no impression on it at all.

Still they kept on trying, until the tips of their fingers were too sore to try any longer. Then they sat back on their heels and considered the problem.

'We need something to dig with,' said Primrose. 'Stones might do.'

They searched under the hedge for stones with sharp edges, and continued digging with these. It was hard work, and they had only managed to widen the gap a little bit when Emerald called them in for their tea.

'Coming!' shouted Bobby.

They watched to make sure Emerald went back into the house; then Primrose whispered urgently, 'Quick! Cover it up with something.'

They broke off bits of hedge and laid them over the gap, then piled soil on top, patting it down until no one could have guessed they had been digging there.

Bobby and Primrose thought Emerald had called them in early; but Pandy was already home, so they knew that the digging must have taken them a lot longer than they had realised. They'd hardly noticed the afternoon passing.

'Well now, did you have a good sleep?' Pandy asked them at tea.

Primrose was about to say that they hadn't slept at all, but Bobby kicked her under the table just in time and said rapidly, 'We slept for hours ... it was great!'

For he suddenly realised that this was their big opportunity — a chance for adventures beyond anything they'd ever imagined before.

– 7 –

The Treasure Chest

Next morning they continued their work behind the hedge. Primrose had brought along two old table knives from the kitchen. They weren't at all sharp, but they were good and sturdy for digging.

By dinnertime they had chipped away the edge of the moat to leave a wide gap that either of them could slip through easily. The moat sloped a bit on their side — getting down to the bottom wouldn't be much of a problem. They carefully covered up the hole again, and patted the earth flat, before going in for dinner.

'Well,' said Emerald, 'are you going to sleep up the Tree-house again today — or maybe you're tired of it already?'

'No.'

'No!'

Bobby and Primrose answered together, and Pandy and Emerald laughed.

'That was a great idea of yours, Emerald,' Pandy said. 'I've never seen two children so anxious to take a nap.'

Starlight chuckled and clapped her hands.

'Maybe we'll send Starlight up for her nap too.'

Primrose and Bobby were horrified, until they realised that Pandy was only joking.

After dinner, having warned Pandy and Emerald not to disturb them, they raced to the Tree-house and pulled the curtains firmly. They watched the house until they were sure no one was looking out; then they slid quickly down the slide and hid themselves in the hedge.

They waited a few minutes to see if anyone had spotted them, then moved along to the place where they had dug their gap.

Primrose slipped through first, climbing easily to the bottom. It would have been fun to slide, but that would have dirtied her clothes too much and Emerald might have asked questions. Bobby followed, having first broken off a large, leafy bit of hedging to cover the gap behind them.

They stood at the bottom of the moat and looked around with gleeful faces.

The fence was behind them, and far above their heads. They walked forward across the bottom of the moat. In front of them, like the strangest mountain you could possibly imagine, the Sandwich of rubbish soared to massive heights. It went straight up, for all the world as if it had been cut with a giant knife.

'How did they get the edge so even?' asked Primrose.

'I dunno.' Bobby was puzzled too.

They looked around. To the right, the Sandwich continued unbroken around the corner of their garden; but to the left there was a narrow ramp of soil set into it, leading up from the moat.

'We can get up that way.' Bobby nodded towards the ramp.

'No! Not today. Let's climb the Great Sandwich Mountain first. I want to see what's in the case.'

Primrose pointed far overhead to where the suitcase could be seen, sticking out slightly. It was surrounded by rubble and lumps of concrete. The bit that faced out was long and narrow, with no handle, so they knew that it was just the bottom of the case, and that most of it was buried in the Sandwich.

Bobby's eyes lit up. 'Buried treasure?'

Primrose nodded. 'Right!' She grinned and closed her eyes tightly, to get into the spirit of the thing. 'I see diamonds and opals,' she chanted, 'strings of shining pearls of greatest price, golden goblets rimmed with precious stones, bangles all encrusted with rubies....'

Primrose was enjoying herself.

'Or it could be full of gold bars from a bank vault,' Bobby said excitedly.

'No.' Primrose opened her eyes and shook her head. 'They would be too heavy. The case wouldn't be strong enough.'

'Then banknotes from a robbery! Hidden by desperate criminals in a house that collapsed — and the rubble was taken to the dump, so they could never find it again. There's a reward of a million pounds for the finder, so we'll be rich for the rest of our lives!'

They stood staring up at the case, a whole world of possibilities just over their heads.

They started to climb.

It was harder than it looked. Although there were plenty of handholds and footholds, they were mostly soft at this point, not firm, and they found themselves slipping to the bottom again with relentless regularity. Bobby clung to a plastic bag and a piece tore away in his hands. Primrose discovered that standing on a perfectly good piece of timber could make it crumble into dust. Bits of soil sprinkled down on them, making things generally uncomfortable.

After they'd fallen to the bottom for the millionth time, it seemed easier to remain there. Tired and disappointed, they viewed the Great Sandwich Mountain in exasperation.

'It looks so easy,' said Bobby.

Primrose sighed. 'All the best mountains are like that, Emerald says, until you try to climb them. We'll have to think it out a bit better — plan our route, the way real mountaineers do.'

They were sitting on the bottom of the moat, trying to figure out the best way up, when they heard Emerald's voice calling.

'Bobby! Primrose!'

They jumped to their feet and raced across to the slope, scrabbling their way frantically back up to the fence, before shouting as loudly as they could:

'Coming!'

'Coming!'

They could see Emerald standing by the back door. She went inside when they answered, and they sighed with relief. Quickly they slipped back under the fence and concealed the gap again with branches and soil.

When they reached the house, they saw that they had a visitor.

'Great-Aunt Holly has come for tea,' said Emerald. Then she frowned. 'What on earth have you two been up to? Look at the state of your clothes! I thought you were in the Tree-house?'

It was only then that Bobby and Primrose realised just how dirty they were.

Emerald sighed. 'Off you go and wash, and change into something clean. You can't hug Great-Aunt Holly looking like that.'

Great-Aunt Holly laughed. 'It's only good clean dirt.'

'Oh no it's not!' said Emerald firmly. 'Not here. If it were, I wouldn't mind.' She turned to the children.

'Hurry up, now — you use the bath, Bobby, and Primrose can have the shower.'

So they went to wash the Sandwich Mountain dirt off themselves before joining Great-Aunt Holly in the sitting-room. There they had to answer endless questions about school, and keep an eye on baby Starlight, while Pandy and Emerald prepared a nice tea.

— 8 —

Great-Aunt Holly

'How do you climb a difficult mountain?' Bobby asked suddenly, right in the middle of the meal.

Pandy and Emerald didn't seem surprised. All sorts of things were discussed at the Scrabblemongers' tea-table.

'Well,' said Emerald, feeling this was her territory more than Pandy's, 'there are different types of mountain-climbing. There's hill-walking, and rock-climbing, and then there are high mountains. Those are more difficult: you have to have oxygen, and supply teams, and camps at various levels, to help you get up there.'

'I know all about that,' said Great-Aunt Holly firmly. 'There isn't a person in the world knows more about that than me. Used to have a mountaineering sweetheart in my younger days. Brought me climbing many a time.'

Bobby and Primrose stared.

Great-Aunt Holly had never got married, and had owned a bakery before she retired. She was plump and homely-looking, as if she had spent her whole life baking buns. It came as a surprise to the two of them that Great-Aunt Holly could have had any other sort of life at all — and the very thought of her swinging from a rope on a high mountain peak was so novel that, for a moment, they were quite speechless.

Emerald just smiled.

Finally Primrose said, 'What happened to him — your sweetheart? Why didn't you marry him?'

'Avalanche,' said Great-Aunt Holly sadly. 'On Mount Everest. Swept him clean away. Never even found the body. Still up there. Frozen in the snow forever.' She sighed. 'Ah, well — it would have pleased him to know Mount Everest was to be his final resting-place.'

Primrose and Bobby were wide-eyed as they looked at Great-Aunt Holly in a completely new light. She had gone all silent, thinking about her lost sweetheart.

'But how do you actually climb a mountain?' Bobby said at last.

Great-Aunt Holly came out of her trance and considered the question. 'Got to have equipment — proper boots, and ropes for the dangerous bits. And there are ways of doing things and ways of not doing things. You must use your head as much as your feet. Very important, that. Can't go far without a head.'

'No, indeed,' said Emerald. 'I'm always telling them that.'

Great-Aunt Holly nodded, but she started looking around restlessly, as if she was going to change the subject.

'What about soft stuff?' asked Primrose quickly.

'Soft stuff?'

'Soft mountains, like bog or ... or snow, where you can't get a proper grip.'

'Bogs? Oh, bogs you avoid like the plague. Could disappear forever. Had a friend who did just that. One minute he was there, then the next minute ... squelch! He was gone!' Great-Aunt Holly helped herself to a slice of freshly baked chocolate sponge.

'Well, snow, then,' Primrose said. 'Snow on a steep mountain slope.'

'Nasty stuff, that! Got to treat it with respect. Shifts around, it does. Never know what it covers until you stand on it, then — whoosh! You're gone! Down a bottomless crevasse. Happened to me once, but I was lucky: roped to my sweetheart, and he was able to haul me up again. In the Himalayas, it was. Very cold. Got a bit of frostbite on my nose that time, too. Look!' She pointed to her nose.

Great-Aunt Holly had a small and rather flat nose. Who would ever have believed that she had lost some of it to frostbite?

Bobby stared at her. He was rather alarmed by his great-aunt's sudden change of status — from dull old

51

Holly, who enquired about school and gave them pencil-cases for their birthdays, to a daring mountaineer who even had the battle-scars to show for it. He felt a bit like Alice in Wonderland, where people weren't quite what they seemed.

Primrose, however, refused to be sidetracked. She was still thinking in a straight line.

'How do you *grip* snow, for climbing? How do you stop yourself sliding back down the mountain again?'

Great-Aunt Holly looked at her thoughtfully, then said, 'Crampons and ice picks. Crampons are spikes that you tie to your boots — bite into the snow and ice and stop you slipping. Ice picks do the same. You tie them to a rope, clip the rope to your belt, and off you go!'

'More tea, Holly?'

'Yes, please. That's the nicest cup of tea I've had in ages.' She held out her cup to Emerald.

'It's Darjeeling — Pandy and I like it very much. It's a little bit dear, but worth it. Nothing beats a good cup of tea.'

'I agree,' said Great-Aunt Holly. 'Some of the stuff you buy nowadays is just dross, pure dross — dust from the bottoms of the tea-sacks. Tastes terrible.'

So the conversation changed from mountains and snow and crampons and ice picks to an argument about tea versus tea-bags. Great-Aunt Holly went into a long complaint about round tea-bags, which she didn't like one bit.

'Bags have corners,' she said. 'Who ever heard of a bag without corners? Tea from them doesn't taste the same, either. Doesn't taste the same at all!'

Primrose and Bobby yawned. Conversation was back to Great-Aunt Holly's normal style, and try as they might, they couldn't manage to swing it back again to a more exciting subject.

– 9 –

Crampons and Ice Picks

'What can we use?' asked Primrose. 'Think! We need ice picks and crampons.'

The two of them thought hard. It was difficult; Pandy and Emerald were careful about sharp objects around the house.

'What about a grater?'

'There's only one' — Primrose shook her head — 'and we can't squash Emerald's grater, anyway — she needs it.'

They thought some more. Then Primrose had a brilliant idea.

'I know: forks! All those old ones in the kitchen drawer. They've gone too shabby to use, Emerald says. We could tie them underneath our trainers for crampons.'

That was half of the problem solved; but, try as they might, they couldn't think of anything suitable for ice picks. It was a few days before the rest of the problem was solved, and Pandy was the one to solve it.

'Look what I've got,' he said, coming into the kitchen. 'Tom found them. Thought they might be useful.'

He had a plastic bag full of things that rattled. He shook them out onto the table.

'Shelf brackets. Fine big strong ones, too.'

Emerald picked one up and examined it. The bracket was metal and L-shaped; the long side measured about nine inches, the short side about half of that, and there were small holes here and there for screws. The ends tapered to gently rounded points, with a hole punched in each. Emerald was smiling as she said, 'We can have some new bookshelves now.'

Primrose and Bobby were smiling too, but for a different reason. They looked at the shelf brackets and saw only one thing — ice picks.

'They even have holes in the ends,' whispered Primrose, 'for tying on ropes.'

They were perfect.

'Could we have some to put up a shelf in the Tree-house?' asked Bobby.

'I'll do it for you,' offered Pandy.

'No. It's OK. We want to do it ourselves.'

Pandy laughed, and handed them two of the brackets. 'I'll keep an eye out for some wood,' he said. 'Hold on to those in the meantime.'

Hold on to them they did, hardly able to believe their good luck. They now had all the equipment they needed.

They raced down to the Tree-house and swung up the rope ladder, each clutching a precious ice pick. Bobby rifled through the bits and pieces they had in the chests and found what he was looking for — a long piece of orange rope left over from the clothesline.

With great difficulty they cut it in half, sawing with the old table knives and their cutting-out scissors. Then, taking a piece each, they set about threading the rope through their shelf brackets.

'It's too thick!' Bobby pushed and pushed, but the rope broke up into four strands and only one went through the hole.

'It would do if we could get even two of the strands through,' Primrose said. 'Then we could tie them in a knot with the other two.'

'Two won't go! They get all jammed up.' Bobby was impatiently mangling the end of his rope against the hole.

It seemed impossible until Primrose suggested glue. 'Stick the ends into a hard bit, like shoelaces. When it's dry it might go through.'

And so it did. They now had two sturdy ice picks.

A further root in the chests produced two belts, which they buckled around their waists. They tied on the free ends of the ropes — and eventually stuck the brackets in their belts too, as otherwise they hung down and banged off their ankles.

And that was that.

The crampons weren't quite so successful. Bobby and Primrose tied the forks to their trainers with strips of old cloth, but it was hard to get them to stay exactly where they were meant to. And when they tried walking, the forks kept turning over so the prongs faced up instead of down. But, with a combination of rag-strips and sellotape, they eventually got it right.

The best way, they discovered, was to tie the forks in place, then put on the trainers, and secure the whole lot with sellotape wound around trainers, forks and ankles. Of course, it meant that they would have to cut the trainers off again — but they had a good supply of sellotape, and at least the crampons were firm and secure that way.

'I feel like I'm wearing real climbing boots,' said Bobby, clumping around the Tree-house.

'Mine even *look* like real climbing boots.' Primrose was examining her own feet with interest.

They sat on the bunks and surveyed their equipment with satisfaction — real mountaineers at last!

Now they were ready to tackle the Great Sandwich Mountain.

– 10 –

Climbing the Great Sandwich Mountain

They picked an afternoon when Emerald had gone to town and Pandy was busy minding Starlight. This was to make sure they wouldn't be called in for visitors again. Whatever about coming in dirty, appearing with forks sellotaped to the bottoms of their shoes would take a great deal more explaining.

They pulled the curtains in the Tree-house and set to work. Getting the crampons right required a lot of concentration, and Primrose had a pain in her middle from bending down before she was finished.

Bobby got the ice picks out of his chest, and they secured them to their belts. They looked at each other silently. It was time to go.

'Wait! We're going to have a ceremony,' Primrose said. 'To bring us luck.'

She took two eggcups from the windowsill, then pulled a bottle of amber liquid out of her chest.

'What's that?' asked Bobby in surprise.

'Brandy. To fortify us against the frost and snow and the terrible cold, and to prevent us losing our noses to frostbite.'

She poured the liquid into the eggcups and handed one to Bobby. Solemnly they raised the little cups in the air, clinked them together and said, 'Cheers!' Then they downed the contents in one gulp.

Primrose put Starlight's bottle of rosehip syrup back in the chest, and they set off on their great adventure.

Pandy was nowhere to be seen, so they quickly slid down the slide and crawled under the hedge. Through the wire, the Great Sandwich Mountain faced them, with all its secrets and all its perils — and they were going on a dangerous journey to find real buried treasure.

They slipped through the gap beneath the fence and eased themselves down the slope. Slowly, awkwardly, they made their way across the bottom of the moat. It was difficult to walk with the forks under their trainers, and they wanted to be sure not to dislodge them. So they went along with a clumping, up-and-down movement.

'This must be like walking on the moon,' Bobby decided, 'in all that deep moon-dust.'

'Well, I'm glad we don't have to carry oxygen!' Primrose felt she had quite enough to cope with as it was.

At last they reached the base of the Great Sandwich Mountain.

They stood there, looking up at the Treasure Chest with mounting excitement. In just a few minutes they'd be up there too, getting it open. What would they find? The anticipation almost made them feel dizzy.

However, it took a great deal longer than a few minutes.

The crampons gripped very well, but it was hard work. Primrose and Bobby got into quite a sweat, pulling and pushing, and craning their necks back to find the best places to dig in with their ice picks. They were distracted, too, by all sorts of interesting objects on the way up.

Primrose found a nice blue vase that looked like it might be intact. But it was firmly jammed in the wedge of rubbish, and she couldn't pull it out. Bobby found a black watch that might only need a new battery, but he reluctantly shoved it back; Emerald would only want to know where he'd got it. There was a dried bunch of flowers that fell to pieces when Primrose attempted to pull it out, and a pile of cockleshells painted different colours. Everything was layered through with soil, which fell on top of them every time they dug their ice picks into a new position.

Slowly they made their way up the Sandwich Mountain. Primrose was first to reach the Treasure Chest. She wedged her ice pick in firmly overhead, and used it for support while she pulled at the case with her free hand.

'It's stuck tight!' she called to Bobby, who was still only three-quarters of the way up. He'd met a particularly soft patch and had to detour around it.

'Rock it free!' he shouted.

Primrose tried to rock the case, but it wouldn't budge. She gave it a thump with her fist. A rattling sound came from inside, and Primrose let out a screech.

'Did you hear that? Did you hear?'

Bobby had heard.

He was now at the same level as Primrose, digging in with his ice pick. When it felt secure he turned, holding on with one hand. They stared at the case, their hearts beating fast with excitement.

Bobby thumped the case again. The sound was quite clear, a metallic shifting, as if the case was full of....

'Gold coins!' breathed Primrose.

'Pieces of eight!' whooped Bobby.

They thumped the case again and again, and each time the sound was the same. They set to digging it out.

But the case wouldn't budge.

They spent ages poking around it with their fingers and not getting very far, as it was surrounded by concrete rubble, which was jammed tight. They pushed and pulled at the smaller lumps, rocking them backwards and forwards and sideways, without managing to dislodge a single piece.

They held on to bigger pieces of concrete and used their ice picks for digging, but it made no difference at all. They thumped the case in frustration and it rattled its gold coins at them, tantalising.

Bobby and Primrose were exhausted. Their arms ached from hanging on to the ice picks, and their toes were numb from pressing down hard on the forks. Bobby had broken a fingernail, and it was sending out jabs of pain. Primrose pressed her face against the Treasure Chest and almost cried with the frustration of being so near, and yet so far from, the clinking gold.

Finally, they had to admit defeat.

They climbed slowly down again, and sat at the bottom of the Sandwich Mountain to recover. The disappointment was unbearable, and left them silent for once.

After a while, they got up and clumped their way back across the moat to the slope. Even the slope was difficult to climb now, as their arms and legs were so desperately tired. They crawled under the fence, and shoved the branches and soil dejectedly over the opening again.

Back in the Tree-house, they removed all the sellotape with cutting-out scissors, which took a long time, and untied the rags that bound the forks to their trainers. Bobby stored the ice picks and ropes and crampons in a corner of his chest, and slowly shut the lid on all their dreams.

They would have to try again another day.

— 11 —

Pandy

When Primrose was first learning how to write, her teacher had asked the class to do a line or two on the subject of 'My Daddy'.

They were mostly predictable:

'My daddy wears glasses and a shirt.'

'My daddy smokes a pipe and reads his paper.'

'My daddy shaves every day and goes to the office.'

But Primrose had simply written:

'My daddy makes cakes.'

For this was true — and oh, what cakes!

Pandy could make anything: castles, trains, flowers, faces, clowns, animals — you name it, and he could make it.

For Emerald's birthday, he had made her a cake in the shape of a mountain peak, with a blue lake at the bottom surrounded by little pine trees.

For Primrose's last birthday it had been a huge beef-burger. The bun part was made of chocolate sponge, with a sprinkling of sunflower seeds baked into the top half. The beefburger itself was a Rice-Krispie-and-chocolate mixture shaped into a circle. There was a lot of work to be done on this cake, so Pandy needed help.

While he was busy baking the sponge and doing the Rice-Krispie bit and making butter icing, Bobby and Primrose rolled out a block of marzipan. They did this with a rolling pin, as if it were pastry. Then they cut two big squares of it to drape over the beefburger, for cheese. After that, they stamped out lots of marzipan circles with eggcups. When they each had a pile of golden discs in front of them, Primrose fetched the little bottles of red and green food-colouring and two paintbrushes kept specially for the purpose.

This was the bit they liked best.

Bobby dipped his brush into the red colouring and carefully painted around the edge of each of his circles. Then he painted spokes into the centre, and little dots for seeds. They looked exactly like tomato slices.

Primrose painted all her circles green, for cucumber. Then she squeezed the leftover bits of marzipan together into a ball and rolled it flat again. This time she cut large teardrop shapes, and carefully stretched the edges to give them a frilly look. Painted green, this was lettuce.

When the sponge was ready, everything was sand-wiched inside it with butter icing.

The final bit was so popular that Primrose and Bobby fought over doing it. Pandy made up bright-red runny icing, and they dribbled it over the burger bun so that it ran down the sides like tomato sauce. It was all great fun, and the whole thing looked nearly too good to eat when it was finished.

Once, when Primrose and Bobby were sick in bed with measles, Pandy had baked a sponge with white icing on top. Then he drew a face on the cake and stuck red cherries all over it, for measles, which made the two of them laugh so much that they felt a bit better and were even able to eat a tiny slice each.

Of course, cakes cost money, and the Scrabblemongers didn't have much. So the way Pandy managed was this: every time he was paid for an odd job, he would buy something small — a bottle of food-colouring, or some flavouring, or a packet of icing sugar, or a bar of cooking chocolate. Then, whenever he wanted to make a special cake, the ingredients were already there.

He came home one afternoon with packets of marzipan, having just completed three days' work, and said to Bobby and Primrose, 'How about a cake?'

It was shortly after their failed attempt to get the Treasure Chest. Emerald had reported that they were moping about, which was most unlike them, and Pandy thought a cake might help.

'But it's not anybody's birthday!' Bobby said.

Pandy laughed. 'Let's just call it a surprise cake. Now ... what do you want?'

Primrose looked at Bobby, and Bobby looked at Primrose, and without the slightest hesitation they both said, 'A treasure chest!'

Pandy was astonished that they had both thought of the same thing at exactly the same time. He didn't know, of course, that they had thought of little else for days.

So Pandy made a deep, square chocolate sponge. When it was cool, he carefully cut off the top for a lid. Primrose hollowed out the base a bit with a spoon — enough for it to hold treasure — and put it on a silver tray. Pandy covered the cake with chocolate butter icing, then wiped the back of his hand across his forehead and said, 'Phew! This is hard work!'

'It's OK, Pandy,' Primrose said. 'You go and have a cup of tea. We can do the rest.'

'You're sure?'

'We're sure!'

'Great kids!' Pandy grinned, and went to switch on the kettle.

Bobby and Primrose rolled out the marzipan.

Using a coin each, they pressed them into the marzipan again and again, until there were coin-prints all over its surface. Then they cut out the rounds, using bottle-tops of the correct size. They made piles and piles of coins, and heaped them into the treasure chest until it was nice and full.

'Treasure isn't treasure unless there's loads and loads of it,' Bobby declared.

Primrose was frowning at the chest. 'There should be jewels, too.... Pandy, have you any white icing — the stuff you roll out?'

Pandy looked up from his cup of tea and waved a hand towards the store cupboard. 'Help yourself to whatever you need.'

Primrose took out a packet of ready-to-roll icing and broke off bits to colour red and blue, for rubies and sapphires, which she placed in among the marzipan coins. Bobby was busy stamping out more coins, to spill down onto the tray in a heap.

Next Primrose made pearls, rolling the white icing into tiny balls, which she strung together with a needle and thread. These she draped over the other treasure, letting some of the pearls hang down over the side of the treasure chest.

'I must say, that looks really lovely.' Emerald had come in to watch, with Starlight in her arms.

But Primrose wasn't satisfied yet. 'It's not glittery enough.' She looked at the cake with her head to one side, thinking.

'I know! Silver balls!' She ran to the store cupboard and rooted around until she found the tiny silver balls they had used for decorating the Christmas cake. There was over half a box still left, and she poured them into the treasure chest so that they settled in piles between the gold coins and the rubies and sapphires and pearls, catching the light in a most satisfactory way.

They left the lid tilted against the back of the cake, as it proved too difficult to prop it up in a half-open position. But the treasure chest looked beautiful — so beautiful, in fact, that they couldn't bear to eat it.

For three whole days it stood on the sideboard while they all admired it, until Pandy said they'd better get eating before the sponge went stale. So they cut into it for tea.

Starlight loved the marzipan coins, which she examined at great length before eating them; but they had to keep the pearls away from her, as she tried to swallow them, string and all.

By the next evening they had eaten the rest of the cake, and their beautiful treasure chest was gone.

– 12 –

The Scary Scary Monster

Bobby and Primrose were restless for the next few days.

They had been distracted for a while by the cake, but now they couldn't settle down to doing anything. Bitterly disappointed about the Treasure Chest, they still felt unable to face another assault on the Great Sandwich Mountain just yet.

'Do you think real mountaineers feel like this?' asked Primrose. 'You know — when they try to climb a peak and are turned back by snow just before they reach the summit?'

'They couldn't feel much worse,' said Bobby morosely. The Treasure Chest was in his mind night and day. He couldn't stop thinking about it.

They were in the Tree-house, just sitting on the chests, doing nothing in particular. Bobby got up and went to the telescope to have another look at the Treasure Chest. It shot into view through the glass, so close that he felt he could almost put his hand down the telescope and pick it up.

It was unbearable!

He swung the telescope away from the Sandwich with an angry gesture, but continued to stare into it, to conceal the fact that tears had suddenly filled his eyes. Everything had gone blurry. As his eyes cleared, he found he was looking at something very strange moving out on the horizon, in the direction of the ramp.

He stared, then called urgently, 'Primrose! Primrose! Come quickly!'

He stood back and gestured to Primrose to look through the telescope.

'What is it?' she asked after a moment.

'What do *you* think it is?'

'I dunno.... It's weird.'

Out on the skyline, a ragged brown object was loping along, not upright, not crawling, but something in between.

Then, quite suddenly, it disappeared; and though they continued searching for a long time, they didn't see it again.

Until the next morning.

There it was, loping along the skyline once more, this time coming towards them. It looked quite extraordinary — brown and huge and sort of round, with bits of fur or something hanging from its body. It could travel at quite a speed, too ... and it was heading their way!

'Is it an animal?' Bobby shoved the telescope over to Primrose in alarm.

Primrose stared through the glass, adjusting it so that she had a really sharp view as the thing came closer. A horrible thought came into her head. The longer she looked at the shaggy object, and the nearer it got, the more certain she became that her horrible thought was right. She backed slowly away from the telescope, her face very white, and looked at Bobby with wide, frightened eyes.

'It's a Scary Scary Monster!'

Hearts beating fast, they watched it approach, coming nearer and nearer. At the top of the ramp, the monster stopped. It stood still for a minute, seeming to sniff at the air. Then it suddenly turned and went lolloping away, all hunched up, its ragged brown fur blowing around its body like a cape. It disappeared over the horizon and was gone.

Primrose and Bobby clung to each other, shaking with the shock. They didn't know which was worse — the sight of the monster coming towards them, or the realisation that it was probably still there — waiting — just out of sight....

'Do you think it saw us?' Primrose asked fearfully.

'Something frightened it off,' said Bobby.

'It was so close that time.' Primrose shivered. 'Do you think it'll come back?'

The question was left hanging in the air as they kept vigil by the window. But the monster was gone — for the moment.

— 13 —

Trailing the Scary Scary Monster

They watched it for days.

It never came so near again, just pottered along the skyline. They couldn't figure out what it was doing.

They were quite sure, however, about it being a monster. It wasn't an animal — not one they knew about, anyway — and it certainly wasn't human. And it wasn't a ghost, either — it was right there in front of them. They could see it quite clearly. If it wasn't an animal, or human, or a ghost, then it could only be a monster.

'A prehistoric monster,' breathed Bobby, watching it one day. 'It's a prehistoric monster that's come out of the depths of the dump ... out of some deep hole that goes down to the centre of the earth.'

'Like the Loch Ness monster,' Primrose nodded, 'only it comes out of a watery hole.'

Somehow, watching the thing mooching about every day made it seem less alarming, especially since it always went back where it came from. Within a couple of weeks they had got quite used to it — even curious to know more.

Primrose started the whole thing.

'Do you think it lives over there ... somewhere we could *see*?'

When Bobby realised what she was saying, he burst out, 'We couldn't!' He looked shocked.

Primrose was silent for a moment; then she said, 'Pity, though, isn't it? The monster might disappear again for good at any minute, and we'll wonder for the rest of our lives if maybe it was a great scientific discovery that would have made us famous. Emerald says we should always find out about things.'

'I don't think she meant this sort of thing, exactly!'

But Primrose had planted the seed, and gradually the idea took hold, until Bobby finally agreed that it would be positively unscientific of them not to investigate the monster while the chance was there.

They fixed on an afternoon when they were meant to be sleeping in the Tree-house, and agreed that, if the monster appeared early enough, they would follow it to its lair.

The first day they sat waiting, the monster never appeared at all, and they couldn't decide whether they were disappointed or relieved. But two days later, there it was — travelling along the skyline with its ungainly gait. They watched it for some time as it circled around; then it disappeared over the horizon again.

Primrose felt her mouth go dry, and Bobby was holding his breath, but the monster didn't reappear.

They stood there, prickling with fear now that the moment had come.

Primrose finally said it. 'Let's go!'

They slid down the slide and raced for the hedge, pushing underneath to the spot where the gap was covered up. Quickly, before their courage could fail them, they scrabbled the branches and soil to one side and slipped down the slope into the moat.

They raced towards the ramp. Up they went, at a run. When they reached the top, they found themselves running over grass and weeds and rough soil. Further on they came to a pit — a wide, shallow depression in the ground, which led to a slight hill; beyond the hill was a whole series of wide, shallow excavations, as if somebody with a giant spade had gone mad digging holes. The ground appeared to be solid here, not filled in with rubbish like the rest of the dump. Primrose and Bobby slithered down into each hole as they came to it and scrambled up the other side, running in the straightest line possible.

The ground levelled out again, and they stopped for a moment to look behind them. They were shocked to discover how far away their house was. They could barely see the roof. The Tree-house seemed tiny, perched up in its tree.

They were shocked by something else, too: the sudden realisation that the monster could easily have sneaked back, and might well have been lying in wait for them in any of the pits they'd so recklessly rushed into on their headlong flight.

Nervously they scanned the landscape around them, searching for more pits, or other places where the monster might be lurking. Nothing looked the same as it did from the Tree-house. It was all scarily unfamiliar. Every rise of the ground was now suspect, every shadow a threat, and help was far, far away. Bobby and Primrose stared uneasily at each other, and for a horrible moment they knew ... that if either of them chickened out, they'd *both* be running home as fast as their legs would carry them.

But the moment passed. Emerald's children were made of sterner stuff than that.

Resolutely, they turned and went on. The ground sloped upwards again. It was stony underfoot, and they slipped and stumbled, even though they had stopped running.

Suddenly, the ground dropped away to a deep gully.

Bobby and Primrose lay flat on the edge and looked down. There was a slope on their side, but the opposite wall of the gully was a cliff of sheer rock. Right at the bottom, resting against the cliff, was a huge piece of concrete piping. It was just sitting there, not connected to anything at all.

'It's really big!' whispered Primrose. 'You could stand inside and not reach the ceiling.'

'It's a sewer pipe,' said Bobby. 'They have big ones like that in cities.'

Stones and planks of wood had been heaped up against one end of the pipe, closing it off. At the other end, something hung across the opening like a curtain, making it impossible to see in.

There was no sign of life.

'Will we go down?' Primrose's voice was wobbly with fear.

Bobby nodded. They'd come too far to turn back.

They crept down the slope of the gully, trying not to dislodge any stones on the way, and stood staring at the sewer pipe.

Nothing stirred.

The place seemed cut off from any sound of the outside world, and there was an unnatural stillness. Not even a whisper of a breeze disturbed the clumps of rough grass growing among the rubble on the gully's floor. They tiptoed over to the sewer pipe and crouched down against its side. Primrose put an ear to the concrete and listened.

'I don't hear anything,' she whispered after a minute.

'Nor do I.' Bobby was shivering.

'It's not there at all!'

'So why are we whispering?'

'Just in case.' Primrose felt her insides crawl with fear as she said the words.

'You'll have to go and look, then,' Bobby hissed.

'You look! You're the eldest.'

'No way!'

'But I'm a girl,' Primrose protested.

'So?'

Primrose made an outraged face at Bobby, but he only stuck out his tongue.

'OK,' she whispered fiercely, 'I'll do it! But you have to back me up.'

They eased themselves into a standing position and, with Primrose going first, edged along towards the front of the pipe. There they stopped to listen again, flattened against the concrete, hearts thumping.

There was no sound.

Primrose put out her hand and, ever ... so ... slowly, began to lift aside the curtain.

'AAAAARRRRRGHHHH!'

A huge, ragged shape hurled itself at them from inside the sewer pipe, howling like a wild beast.

They screamed in terror and ran — back up the slope of the gully — up, up, up, scrabbling and slipping in a hail of stones and fear — down the hill, down, down, to tumble headfirst into a pit — up and running, falling, tripping, sliding, stumbling in and out of one pit after another — on to the next hill, running, running — down into the first pit, colliding, tripping, falling, hysterical — up again and running, running ... back to the edge of their own familiar moat....

Bobby's head was thumping and his breath was coming in short, painful gasps. He felt as if his ribs were cracked. The pain nearly cut him in two.

Primrose was in a bad way too. Her ears were ringing, and her chest was so sore that she thought her lungs were going to burst. She had a stone in her shoe, but, unable to do anything about it, she had to run with the stone grinding into the sole of her foot every time it hit the ground.

They tumbled down into the moat, and frantically scrambled up the slope to the gap in the fence. Here there was complete panic, as they both tried to get through at once. Bobby elbowed Primrose aside and got under the fence first. They raced up the garden and collapsed against the back wall of the house, beneath the kitchen window.

They hadn't looked behind them once. Now they turned to watch the hedge, realising with horror that the gap was still uncovered. They waited to see if the monster would follow them through. If it did, they'd have to dive for the back door and throw themselves on Emerald's mercy.

There was no movement in the hedge.

Primrose and Bobby sat there for a long time, until their hearts had stopped racing, and their chests had stopped hurting, and the panic which had engulfed them subsided at last, leaving them limp and exhausted.

Pandy found them some time later, just sitting, looking out over the garden, hardly able to move.

'What have you two been up to?' he asked, puzzled.

'We're out of breath,' Primrose whispered, 'and really tired.'

Pandy laughed. 'Trying to run a marathon or something?'

Bobby nodded.

'Oh well,' Pandy said, as baby Starlight wriggled in his arms to get down, 'you'd better come in for eats. That'll revive you.'

Primrose and Bobby got up, feeling as if they had indeed run a full marathon, and went in for tea.

– 14 –

Visit to the Dump

A lthough the Scrabblemongers lived beside the County Council tip-head, and bin-lorries passed right by their front gate, their own bins didn't actually get collected. So every week Pandy had to bring their rubbish to the dump. They never had much, anyway — one bag at the most.

Bobby and Primrose loved this trip. During the school term they went in the afternoon, but in the holidays it was always earlier.

'Let us carry it — please, Pandy!' begged Primrose one morning, as Pandy tied the top of the black bag securely.

Pandy picked it up, gauging the weight. He had just finished painting the kitchen chairs, and most of the rubbish consisted of old newspapers that he had put down to protect the floor.

'It's light enough today, all right,' he said. 'I suppose you can.'

Bobby took hold of the top, and Primrose clutched the two bottom corners, and off they went — around to their front gate, and down the road to the gates of the dump. The road ended here. There was a huge notice at the bottom of the cul-de-sac:

COUNTY COUNCIL LANDFILL SITE

There was also a smaller notice, saying:

TIP-HEAD →

Inside the gates were two roads. One went straight ahead to the public dumping area; the other swung right, towards the main tip-head.

Bobby and Primrose hurried straight ahead and shouted 'Hello' to Mr Moneyman, who stood outside his wooden hut. He had a leather bag hanging from a strap that went around his neck and across one shoulder. When she was small, Primrose always used to ask him, 'What's your name?' He would laugh and reply, 'I'm the money-man!' So Mr Moneyman he became.

He was on duty all day; he took the money from people who wanted to use the public dump, giving them a ticket in return. There was a big notice-board beside his hut, listing all the vehicles that could be admitted — cars, small trailers, large trailers, small vans, trucks — and giving the price for each.

He didn't charge Pandy, however, as Pandy was clearly none of those things; but Bobby always felt a bit cheated, as they didn't get a ticket either.

'Going to wash your feet today?' Mr Moneyman chuckled.

It was a fine day, and he had the water hose on to dampen down the dust. Bobby and Primrose slowly walked along beside the hose, with the bin-bag between them, pretending they were a big black car, and squealing as the cold water sprayed their ankles.

'That's right!' Mr Moneyman nodded solemnly. 'Now you won't be messing up my nice clean dump with your dusty old shoes!'

They grinned, and asked him for a look in his money-bag. It was empty. It nearly always was, this early in the day. In the afternoon it would be nice and jingly.

He waved a hand at them. 'Off you go! You'll have me exhausted!' And he went to sit in his little hut.

Pandy and Bobby and Primrose continued up a stony road to the places specially laid out for the public to dump their rubbish. First there was the new recycling bay, with its row of skips to separate various things that would now be re-used in one way or another: timber, metal, cardboard, green garden-waste, newspapers, glass bottles, aluminium cans and textiles. Here an argument started. Bobby wanted to empty their bin-bag into the newspaper skip, but Pandy was worried about all the paint he'd spilt on the papers; he thought the bag should go in the general dump. Primrose agreed with him, so Bobby was outvoted.

They walked on until they came to a wide gravelled area, with a deep trench dug around it on three sides to take the rubbish. The area had a concrete rim, so that cars and vans could safely drive right to the edge and dump their loads. At the end of every day the trench was cleared by bulldozers, so it was nice and clean and ready for another lot of customers the next morning.

Primrose and Bobby stood on the concrete edge and let their bin-bag drop down into the trench. It bumped and somersaulted all the way to the bottom, where it lay like a big fat slug. The trench was completely empty — apart from what they'd just put in.

But there were seven fridges in the special wired-off compound at the entrance to the gravelled area. Fridges had to stay there until somebody came to release the gas from their systems; then they could safely be buried. Primrose pressed her nose to the wire, feeling vaguely sorry for them. Primrose felt sorry for anything that was caged in.

'They'll be gone by evening,' Pandy said. 'The gas-man comes today.'

They walked back down the road. Crows were picking around on the ground beside the path. Bobby and Primrose looked at each other and grinned; then they ran at the crows, with their arms waving in the air, and shouted, *'Begone!'* The crows rose up into the air, cawing in panic.

'Don't do that!' Pandy was a bit annoyed with them. 'The birds aren't doing any harm at all.'

'They like it,' said Primrose. 'It's a game.'

The crows settled back on the ground behind them as they walked towards the gates.

The County Council offices were right beside Mr Moneyman's hut. Mr John often waved to the Scrabblemongers from his window. There was no sign of him today, however.

They were near the road to the main tip-head, and Bobby and Primrose raced each other to it.

Here there was another, much larger, hut. In front of it, set into the ground, was a huge metal plate, big enough for the biggest truck or lorry to park on. This was really a giant weighing-scale called a weighbridge. All commercial traffic was weighed, as firms were charged by the tonne for dumping rubbish at the tip-head; the weights registered inside the hut. Even the County Council's own bin-lorries were weighed, for the purpose of statistics.

Primrose and Bobby reached the weighbridge together, but Primrose let Bobby go first.

He stood on the metal plate and shouted, 'What do I weigh?'

Mr Charlie Checker was sitting by the window. He looked at his register and said, 'Five tonnes! *You'll* cost a pretty penny to dump!'

'You're not dumping me!' Bobby yelled, and ran as Charlie pretended he was coming out to catch him.

Primrose was already standing on the big metal plate.

'And what do I weigh?' she demanded.

Mr Charlie Checker frowned at his register, then looked at Primrose in alarm. 'Twenty tonnes! What *have* you been eating since last week?'

Primrose giggled. 'How much will I cost, then?'

'All your pocket money for the next year!'

'I haven't *got* any money.'

'We'll dump you for free, so....' He darted out of the hut, but Primrose was too quick for him and ran off after Bobby, squealing with laughter.

Pandy came over to have a chat with Charlie; but before he could say a word, a line of container lorries rumbled in through the gates, so they had to leave Mr Charlie Checker in peace to do his job.

They went for a walk.

Across the road from the Scrabblemongers' house, and adjoining the dump beyond the bottom of the cul-de-sac, was a field. It belonged to the County Council and was too close to the dump for anything to be done with it, so it was left to run wild.

It was a marvellous place to walk in, even if it was a bit dusty. The grass was waist-high and full of seed-heads and wild flowers. Primrose liked to pick the long stems of grasses. On a good day she could find seven or eight different types.

Bobby and Primrose ran wild themselves here, playing hide-and-seek or 'Sole Survivors of a Plane Crash Crawling Through the Deepest Snake-Infested Jungle'. When they got tired of that, they walked with Pandy to the bottom of the field, where the ground sloped upwards into a hill and overlooked the main tip-head.

They sat on top of the hill and watched the scene below. Lorries and trucks were dumping at the point where the filled-in land stopped, and all the rubbish poured into the remains of the quarry. This area was very busy, and the compactors and bulldozers were hard at work, buzzing to and fro, in and out between the other vehicles. They watched a big lorry tilt its container in the air and empty its load. Bricks and boxes and bags and bits and pieces went bouncing downwards. Other vehicles backed in and released their loads all at the same time, so that rubbish cascaded over the edge with a roar, like a great waterfall.

Bobby was peering down into the quarry, where an excavator was using its long bucket-arm to spread out the rubbish.

'Isn't that dangerous, Pandy? It could get buried!'

Pandy shook his head. 'The driver is careful. Watch how he keeps well away from the loads coming down. He has to know what he's doing, mind.'

Primrose was staring too.

'Pandy, does the quarry go to the centre of the earth?'

'It goes as far as you see, right there in front of you,' Pandy said.

'But are there cracks?'

'Cracks?'

'Cracks that might be a bit covered up, like mountain crevasses covered with snow?'

'No, Primrose. A quarry is a surface mine. It doesn't go underground like a coal mine.'

'But if they had to blast with dynamite to get stuff out of the quarry, there could be a crack, like an earthquake crack.'

Pandy frowned. 'If there is, I've never heard of it.'

'And if there is a crack,' persisted Primrose, 'then a monster might come out of it from the centre of the earth.'

'You've been reading too many stories, young lady!' Pandy laughed.

Bobby had been watching Pandy. Now he asked anxiously, 'Where else could a monster come from?'

'Nowhere,' Pandy said. 'There *are* no monsters.'

'What about the Loch Ness monster — and the yeti?'

'Well, nobody's ever proved that they exist.'

'But if there *was* a monster around here —' Primrose began.

'There isn't,' said Pandy firmly.

'But if there was —'

Pandy looked exasperated. 'What's wrong with you two today? Why all this sudden interest in monsters?'

'We were just wondering,' said Primrose carefully, 'but it doesn't really matter. Race you home, Bobby!'

She got up and ran off down the hill, with Bobby close behind her.

— 15 —

Third Attempt
on the Great Sandwich Mountain

When they had quite recovered from their encounter with the Scary Scary Monster, Bobby and Primrose turned their attention to the Treasure Chest again.

'Let's go this afternoon,' said Primrose one day. They knew by now that Pandy and Emerald never bothered them when they were meant to be asleep in the Treehouse; they would only call them from the back door, if necessary.

'This time,' Bobby said, 'we'll try to cut it open. Pity we don't have a penknife.' Emerald didn't approve of penknives.

They finally settled on the old knives again. These weren't sharp, but they thought that maybe, if they sawed away with them for long enough, they might cut even a little hole in the side of the Treasure Chest, so they could see in.

Then Primrose had an idea.

'What about Pandy's hammer? If we hammered hard enough, we might be able to break through. You know how rotten a lot of the stuff in the Sandwich Mountain is.'

'I'll try and get it,' said Bobby.

Pandy had most of his tools, like chisels and screwdrivers and things with blades, locked away in a special box. But his hammer was on a wall-bracket in the shed.

Bobby managed to slip in and out of the shed unseen, and brought the hammer back to the Tree-house concealed beneath his T-shirt.

'You'll have to carry that,' said Primrose. 'You can stick it in your belt.' Then she quickly added, 'You're bigger than me,' as Bobby looked like he was going to argue. The hammer was very heavy. He opened and shut his mouth, but said nothing in the end.

They took their crampons and ropes and ice picks out of the chest and set to work getting ready.

'It's a nuisance having to do all this,' said Bobby, redoing his forks for the second time as they kept slipping into the wrong position.

'Oh no it's not!' Primrose was decisive. 'Preparation is what matters with everything. Pandy says the same about painting — it's the cleaning and sanding and stuff that takes all the time, not the painting itself. If we were climbing a snowy mountain in the Himalayas, we'd probably have to start planning at least a year ahead.'

She finished winding sellotape around her trainers, then secured her ice pick, while Bobby did the same.

At last they were ready. They dropped down the slide, making sure to land on their heels so as not to dislodge the forks, and crawled under the hedge.

They were horrified to find the gap uncovered — they had forgotten all about it after their last adventure.

'Lucky Pandy didn't spot that,' said Bobby, 'or we'd be in real trouble!'

They squeezed beneath the wire and slid down the slope. They had given up worrying about dirty clothes, since climbing the Sandwich Mountain always left them dirty anyway.

At the bottom of the moat they sat for a few minutes and examined the Sandwich, looking for the best route to the Treasure Chest. Then they clumped across to their chosen starting point for the assault.

Bobby and Primrose stared upwards.

The Treasure Chest was waiting for them, far overhead, sunlight glinting on its rusty rivets. Primrose imagined a hole in its side and a river of coins pouring out, down the face of the Great Sandwich Mountain, like a beautiful golden waterfall. She threw back her arm and dug in with her ice pick, as high as she could reach.

They started to climb.

Side by side they ascended, taking their time, finding the best holds. They made good progress, being experienced mountaineers by now.

'We must be nearly halfway,' said Primrose happily, as they stopped for a rest. Clinging to her ice pick, she looked down to see how far they had come; and as she did, a sudden movement caught the corner of her eye. She turned her head.

To their left, just by the bottom of the ramp, a shaggy brown figure was lurking in the moat. Primrose clutched at Bobby with her free hand and he turned, following her horrified glance.

For a moment the world stood still.

They clung to the side of the Great Sandwich Mountain, frozen with fear, eyes fixed on the apparition before them. The monster didn't seem to have any eyes, or face — or limbs, for that matter, even though it could move. But its menace reached out to them with a stomach-churning closeness.

Bobby gasped, and lost his grip. He grabbed frantically at Primrose, and the two of them tumbled to the ground in a clatter of ice picks. They clung to each other in terror and shock, knowing they couldn't make it to safety this time.

They were trapped!

Hearts thumping wildly, they waited for the monster to come and gobble them up.

The monster moved, but not in their direction. Ever so slowly, it backed away, around the corner where the moat ran up by the side of their garden.

Primrose and Bobby sat, rigid, waiting for its return.

When there was no sign of it after a minute, they frantically scrambled across the moat, half-crawling, half-walking in their panic. They clawed their way up to the gap in the fence, tore through it, and kept going. No way were they risking the Tree-house with the monster lurking in the moat.

They clumped furiously up the garden, like a pair of frenzied astronauts, thumping along with the awkward up-and-down movement that was the only way they could walk at all with the forks stuck to the soles of their trainers. They threw terrified glances at the side hedge, in case the monster climbed over to catch them halfway.

Finally they reached the safety of the house, tripping over themselves in their hurry to get to the back door. They landed on the ground in a tangle.

Emerald had spotted them through the kitchen window. She opened the door and came out, a look of astonishment on her face.

'What on earth ...!'

Her voice trailed off as she saw the forks. Then she started to laugh, and laugh, and laugh.

Pandy came out, carrying baby Starlight, to see what was going on. Emerald pointed, too convulsed even to speak, and Pandy started laughing too.

'What are you *doing* with forks sellotaped to your shoes?' he spluttered.

Bobby was so put out at his parents' laughter that he forgot about the monster.

'They're crampons,' he said indignantly, 'for climbing mountains.'

This sent Emerald and Pandy into a fresh wave of laughter. Pandy recovered enough to lean over and dangle a shelf bracket by its orange rope. 'And what, pray, is this?'

'That's an ice pick,' Primrose answered crossly. It was really mean of Pandy and Emerald to laugh at them like that.

Her answer only made matters worse. Pandy put his arm around Emerald for support as the two of them laughed and laughed and laughed, tears running down their faces with mirth.

Finally, when she'd recovered a bit, Emerald asked, 'What were you going to do — scale the back wall of the house?' and went off into more hysterics of laughter before they could even answer.

'Very funny,' muttered Bobby.

Starlight, bewildered by so much laughter, decided she wanted to get down and join in the fun. She wriggled to be let go, but Pandy, still chuckling, hugged her close and said, 'Not today, lovey. I haven't cleaned the garden. Promise I'll do it some day this week. How about a walk up the fields instead, so you can watch all the nice bulldozers?'

He looked at Bobby and Primrose, a big grin on his face.

'Want to come?'

They nodded. The garden was unusable anyway, while the monster was around, and with Pandy they'd be safe.

– 16 –

Starlight

Baby Starlight was almost a year old, and Emerald liked to let her play in the garden when the weather was fine. This was a lot of trouble, but it was considered worth it, for even babies should have a bit of freedom now and then to explore strange new worlds.

First Pandy had to hoover the grass. He would take Emerald's vacuum cleaner out of its cupboard in the kitchen and plug it into an extension lead, so that he could reach right down to the bottom of the garden. Then he hoovered up the dust that had settled on the grass since Starlight was last out to play.

When the job was done, he produced an armchair for Emerald and a rug for Starlight, which he spread carefully on the nice, newly cleaned grass. Starlight was then placed on the rug, surrounded by all her toys. Emerald would settle herself into the armchair to keep an eye on things.

Baby Starlight might not be able to walk, but boy, could she get around! She was the fastest crawler in the whole world; she could move at the speed of an express train, arms and legs pumping away like pistons in an engine. Even Bobby and Primrose had a job keeping up with her once she got going.

And get going she did, for Starlight was an adventurous soul who shared her mother's thirst for travel. Being a baby, she couldn't normally go anywhere unless she was brought, but the garden was different. As soon as Pandy placed her on the rug she was off, beetling away at top speed down along by the hedge.

She kept to the perimeter until she reached the Tree-house tree. Then she'd stop, reach for the bottom of the rope ladder with one hand and pull herself up until she was swaying unsteadily on her feet, all the time looking upwards to where the Tree-house loomed far overhead.

'That child'll be up that ladder in no time!' Pandy would say, laughing, and Emerald would close her eyes and take a deep breath at the very thought.

Then Bobby and Primrose would put Starlight on the slide, near the bottom, and let her slide gently down all by herself. Squeals of laughter would be followed by demands of 'More! More!' That was the only word Starlight could say, apart from 'Mama' and 'Dada'. When Bobby and Primrose got tired of lifting her onto the slide, off she'd go again, exploring.

She very quickly discovered the places where she could crawl through the hedge so that she was up against the chain-link fence, looking over the moat. She worked her way up and down the garden, sitting in every hidey-hole she could find, testing it for size. When she had gone right around the entire perimeter of the garden and reached the house again, she would climb into Shadow's kennel, which she loved. Once she fell asleep in there, giving Emerald a nasty fright when she couldn't find her.

But Emerald was proud of Starlight, recognising in her a kindred spirit, pushing at the boundaries of her little world. And she had no doubt about one thing: when Starlight grew up, she was going to be a famous explorer too.

One afternoon, Pandy asked Primrose and Bobby to mind baby Starlight. Emerald had gone to town, and Pandy wanted to paint the front of the house, as it hadn't yet had its yearly freshen-up. He had cleaned the garden particularly well that morning, and he knew Starlight would be quite safe as long as somebody was there keeping an eye on her. So he closed the side gate and went around to the front, with his paintbrushes and cans and white spirit and all sorts of other things that have to be kept away from babies.

Primrose and Bobby didn't mind. It was fun looking after Starlight.

They followed her around the garden, laughing at the way she suddenly stopped to examine a daisy in the grass. She poked it with her finger, then put her mouth down and tried to eat it. Bobby had to pull her away quickly, before she got a mouthful.

They made her a daisy-chain and put it around her neck, then made another one for her head and crowned her Princess Starlight. She looked so pretty that they stood admiring her. Starlight basked in their admiration for a couple of minutes before deciding to eat the daisy necklace.

'I'll mind them for you,' said Primrose, taking the daisy-chains off to let Starlight continue her exploring.

They spent ages below the Tree-house. Bobby and Primrose took turns putting Starlight on the slide and swinging her gently on the ladder, making sure to hold her firmly.

Then they went off around the garden again, to Shadow's kennel. Primrose tried to explain to Starlight about Shadow, but she only chuckled and climbed into the kennel, where she peeped out at them with her cheeky little face.

'You're squashing poor Shadow!' Primrose protested, but Bobby said it was OK: Shadow was minding the Tree-house, lying under the slide.

They were having their usual argument about where exactly Shadow was when they heard the sounds of heavy machinery coming closer and closer, then some very strange whooshing noises down at the bottom of the garden.

Primrose ran for the Tree-house, leaving Bobby to follow with baby Starlight. He put Starlight on the grass beside the slide, where she amused herself by putting her bottom on the plank and lifting her legs so that she slid the few inches to the ground.

'Bobby! Bobby! Come quick! Look what they're doing!' Primrose put her head out of the Tree-house door and beckoned. Bobby swung quickly up the ladder.

Primrose was staring out the window, and when Bobby joined her he could see a line of lorries and bulldozers busy at the top of the Great Sandwich Mountain. As they watched, a huge lorry tipped its load over the edge.

'They're filling in our moat!' Bobby's voice was a mixture of astonishment and disbelief.

They watched as load after load was dumped. It all looked like builders' rubble — lumps of cement and bricks and huge slabs of concrete. The bulldozers were busy pushing over any bits that stayed on top of the Sandwich.

'The Treasure Chest!' Primrose let out a loud wail. 'It'll be buried and we'll never see what's in it!'

They looked in horror at the scene before them.

'Maybe we can ask them to stop,' Bobby said.

'They'd never stop. The dump is meant to be none of our business.'

Bobby watched the machinery with a sinking heart, knowing this was true.

But Primrose was thinking hard. 'Bobby,' she said after a couple of minutes, 'if the bottom of the moat is going to rise, then at some stage it'll reach the Treasure Chest — and we'll be able to walk right up to it!'

'I was just thinking that myself,' lied Bobby, annoyed at not having thought of it first.

Then he got a real inspiration of his own. 'We could go at night, if there was a moon — sneak out when Pandy and Emerald are in bed.'

'That's it!' shouted Primrose, and clapped her hands. 'A Moonlight Treasure Hunt!'

They got very excited. This was really something to look forward to. They started to make plans, and they became so engrossed in what they were doing that it was some time before they remembered baby Starlight....

– 17 –

Emergency!

Bobby looked out of the door of the Tree-house, but he couldn't see Starlight anywhere. 'We'd better go down and find her.'

They weren't one bit worried. The garden was safe and secure, even the gap under the fence, which they had remembered to go back and cover after their last adventure.

'She's probably in Shadow's kennel,' said Primrose as they descended the rope ladder.

But Starlight wasn't in Shadow's kennel. They checked the side gate; it was still closed.

'See if Pandy brought her around to the front,' suggested Bobby.

'He wouldn't do that.'

'Check anyway.'

Primrose opened the gate, tiptoed to the corner of the house and peered around it. Pandy had all the windows open and was busy painting the frames.

Primrose came back and closed the gate again. 'She's not there ... must be hiding in the hedges.'

'Well, then,' said Bobby, 'you take this side, and I'll take the other side, and we'll work our way down the garden until we meet at the bottom. She's got to be somewhere.'

So they crawled slowly down the garden, checking every gap in the hedge that went through to the chain-link fence. They even checked the hedge itself, in case she had somehow climbed up into the middle of it — with Starlight, you never knew. But there was still no sign of her as they started to work their way along the bottom hedge.

They met in the middle, and there was just one place left to try. Together they crawled through their own special place in the hedge — and gasped!

The gap beneath the fence, which they had so carefully covered up, was gaping open ... and there, way down in the bottom of the moat, was baby Starlight, crawling along at full speed towards the heap of newly dumped rubble.

'Starlight!'

'*Star-light!*'

Bobby and Primrose shouted together, at the tops of their voices. But Starlight either ignored them or couldn't hear the shouts through the noise of all the machinery overhead. She kept on crawling.

'Look! Look!' screeched Primrose, pointing.

A tipper lorry was backing onto the edge of the Sandwich Mountain, ready to drop its load. It was piled high with blocks and bricks and huge chunks of concrete with vicious-looking wires sticking out from them at all angles.

'Stop! *Stop!*' Bobby and Primrose screamed together. But nobody heard.

Starlight reached the newly dumped rubble and sat down to investigate the wonders spread before her. Directly above, the back of the lorry started rising to tip out its lethal contents.

Bobby fell through the gap at the speed of light. He rolled to the bottom of the moat, and Primrose was already with him as he scrambled up. They raced across the moat towards Starlight, not daring to look overhead.

Reaching Starlight, they grabbed hold of an arm each, hauling her up, then turned and ran ... and ran.... There was a roaring sound, and a shower of stones hit the backs of their legs, almost knocking them down. But they somehow managed to keep going until they reached the slope beneath the gap in the fence. There they collapsed to the ground, breathless, clutching baby Starlight between them.

They looked over towards the Sandwich Mountain. The lorry was now empty, its container standing on end, and there was a huge pile of concrete slabs covering the exact spot where Starlight had been sitting just moments before.

Bobby burst into tears.

He sobbed and sobbed, hugging Starlight tightly. His tears drenched her soft silky hair, dripped down her nose, and plopped onto her plump little hands. She giggled and licked her fingers, liking the salty taste.

Primrose put her arms around both of them, squeezing so hard that Starlight started to squirm in protest. They were in such a state that they didn't notice the commotion above, on the top of the Great Sandwich Mountain.

The poor lorry-driver had spotted them at the exact moment he dumped his load. But it was too late. In complete and utter shock he had watched as the children with the baby tried to run clear. He was sitting on the edge of the Sandwich now, hysterical, with two other lorry-drivers restraining him from jumping straight down in his panic to see if the children were all right. The men came down by the ramp instead, running frantically along the moat to where the little group sat huddled.

Bobby and Primrose and Starlight were hoisted shoulder-high back up to the top of the Sandwich Mountain, and taken to the County Council offices.

●

Pandy got the fright of his life when a bulldozer and a lorry pulled into his driveway, followed by Mr John's car, screeching through the entrance in a shower of gravel. When he saw Bobby and Primrose in the bulldozer, and Starlight on Mr Tom's knees in the passenger seat of the lorry, he dropped his paintbrush, knocked over the can of paint and ran towards his children.

— 18 —

Explanations

There was a huge fuss, of course.

Emerald arrived home to find all kinds of things blocking her driveway, the front lawn splattered with white paint, and her kitchen full of people, most of whom appeared to be crying. Mr John was there, and Mr Tom; so were Mr Boggle and the lorry-driver who'd nearly killed Starlight.

Emerald, practical as ever, switched on the kettle.

Soon she had sorted everyone out with mugs of good hot sweet tea, and made up a comforting bottle for Starlight — who was the only one not really in need of comforting at all. As Starlight snuggled up to Emerald with her bottle, and they all gradually recovered from the shock of what had happened, Bobby and Primrose had to make their explanations.

Pandy and Emerald were horrified.

'You've been playing in the dump all this time! No more! I can tell you that for sure!' Pandy looked grim.

'I can't believe it!' Emerald shook her head. 'In spite of all our warnings, too.'

'Well,' said Mr John, 'it's probably just as well we're closing the dump, so.'

'Closing the dump?' Primrose and Bobby spoke together, astonished.

Mr John nodded. 'That's right. Dumping will finish for good soon. All the remaining bits will be levelled out. We only have to fill in the trench around your house and a big gully over that way.' He waved his hand vaguely in the direction of the ramp.

A flicker of alarm ran through Primrose.

'Will you bury the monster?' The words were out before she realised what she was saying.

There was a sudden silence. Everyone was staring at her.

'What monster?' asked Mr John carefully.

'The one that lives in the big pipe.'

Mr John glanced at Mr Boggle and Mr Tom before turning back to Primrose. Very slowly he said, 'You'd better tell us.'

So Primrose had to explain all about their journey across the pits to the lair of the Scary Scary Monster, and the way he had lain waiting in the moat to frighten them.

Pandy and Emerald were looking quite faint by now.

But Mr John only looked sad.

'So old Mr Popplehanger's back again,' he said softly. 'I didn't know. We'd probably have found him anyway, but it's just as well you told us.'

He was quiet for a moment, then went on to explain: 'He keeps coming back to the dump, he does. Every so often the social workers come and take him to a hostel in the city. Sometimes he stays a while, but he always comes back here in the end.'

'Our monster doesn't *look* like a man,' said Primrose doubtfully.

'Oh, he's a man, all right.'

'Do you allow him to live in the dump?' Bobby was curious.

'Certainly not! Most certainly not! But we don't always notice him. Last time he hid for months in an old wardrobe.... So it's a sewer pipe this time! He's very clever at keeping out of our way when he wants to.'

'What does he eat down there?' asked Primrose, concerned.

Mr John rolled his eyes upwards. 'Heaven only knows!'

'Doesn't he have a family?'

'We don't know.'

'Does he talk?'

'Not much. There's one social worker he likes — isn't that so, Tom?'

Mr Tom nodded in agreement. 'Aye. She's the one who has to come and take him away. He won't go for anyone else. She sometimes gets him to talk a bit. Reckons he's an educated chap. But he never gives any details about his life, or how he came to be living like this.'

'He'll have to be moved for good now,' Mr John said. 'I'll notify the Social Services right away.'

'Can we see him?' asked Primrose anxiously. 'To make sure you've got the right monster?' She was still worried about the possibility of him being buried alive.

Mr John smiled at her concern. 'We'll see,' he said. Then he looked at his watch. 'It's time we were getting back to work.'

He got up to make his departure, and Pandy and Emerald thanked him and Mr Tom and Mr Boggle again, and apologised once more to the poor lorry-driver for his dreadful experience. They waved goodbye from the side gate.

When all the fuss had died down, Bobby and Primrose got off very lightly indeed, because everyone was so relieved that Starlight had come to no harm. But that was the end of their ramblings, for Pandy went out before tea and firmly secured the gap in the fence with half a roll of chicken-wire. When he'd finished, it wasn't even possible to crawl through the hedge at that point any more.

– 19 –

Goodbye to the Scary Scary Monster

The very next morning, a big car pulled up outside the Scrabblemongers' house and blew its horn.

Two men were in the front. A pretty lady with long red hair climbed out of the back and waited with the car door open. Pandy called for Bobby and Primrose to come quickly, and brought them out to the front gate to meet the lady.

When they got to the car, they could see something in the back seat. It looked like a pile of old brown sacks.

'It's the Scary Scary Monster!' breathed Bobby.

The lady smiled and said, 'Mr Popplehanger, the children want to meet you.'

Bobby and Primrose stared at the pile of sacks, which didn't move.

'Come on, Mr Popplehanger,' the lady pleaded. 'The children were worried about you. They want to make sure you're all right. Take that thing off your head for a minute!'

A dirty hand emerged from the pile and reached for the topmost sack. Slowly it pulled the sack to one side, and a face emerged — two very blue eyes, encased in wild and dirty hair, and a beard that seemed to cover most of the rest of the man.

'Hello,' said Bobby.

Primrose smiled. 'Hello, Mr Popplehanger.'

He stared at them blankly, without any sign of recognition, and there was a long silence.

At last Primrose turned to the lady. 'What are you going to do with him?'

'*Do* with him!' The lady laughed. 'We're going to bring him someplace where he can have a nice hot bath, and a nice warm bed, and a change of clothes, and good hot meals, and people to talk to.'

Primrose looked at Mr Popplehanger, who was still staring at them with those blank eyes, and suddenly she felt infinitely sad — sad that he really didn't want all those nice things being offered, and would prefer to live by himself in a rubbish dump. On the spur of the moment she climbed into the car, threw her arms around Mr Popplehanger, and kissed him.

He smelt terrible. She backed out again, keeping the smile on her face, which was very difficult because of the indescribable odour that now clung to her.

Mr Popplehanger continued to stare, but now his eyes were focused on Primrose. A big tear welled up in one of his eyes, tumbled slowly out, and splashed down along his beard.

Primrose was horrified.

'He'll be fine!' The lady squeezed her gently on the shoulder and smiled. Then she got into the car beside Mr Popplehanger and closed the door. The car moved off.

'Goodbye!' shouted Primrose and Bobby. 'Goodbye!'

Then they saw his face. Mr Popplehanger had turned and was staring at them through the back window.

They waved and waved, until the car disappeared out of sight.

– 20 –

Treasure

They were so sad about Mr Popplehanger that they forgot about the Treasure Chest until the next morning. But it was the first thing Primrose thought of when she woke up.

She ran to Bobby's room and shook him awake. 'Bobby! Bobby!'

'What's wrong? What's wrong?' He rubbed the sleep out of his eyes as he struggled to wake up.

'The Treasure Chest!'

'What about it?' He looked at Primrose in alarm.

'We have to get to it quickly. Make plans.'

Bobby sat up in bed. 'Oh, that. You scared me. I thought somebody had stolen it in the night.'

'Don't be silly.'

'It's not silly. Have you looked?'

'I know it's still there. I can *feel* it.' Primrose tucked herself in under the duvet, at the foot of the bed. 'How are we going to get to it, now that Pandy's blocked off the hole?'

They sat and thought about the problem.

'We could climb the fence with our crampons and ice picks,' said Bobby, but the suggestion was half-hearted.

Primrose said nothing, thinking of Starlight and how lucky they'd been. Maybe it was wrong to tempt fate.

Bobby was thinking the same thing. 'We should have told the men the other day,' he said ruefully, 'when we were telling everything else.'

Primrose shook her head. 'It wouldn't have been the right time. We were in enough trouble.'

'We could get Pandy to ask Mr Tom.'

'Pandy would go mad! He doesn't want to hear any more about the dump from us.'

'If Shadow was a real dog, we could tie a note to his collar and send him to Mr Tom with a message.' Bobby looked glum. 'Maybe we could shout to the men from the Tree-house....'

'They'd never hear us. Look what happened with Starlight.' Indeed, shouting had been of little use then.

'Mr Tom's coming for dinner today,' Primrose said suddenly. 'I heard Emerald say so. If we got him on his own....'

Bobby's eyes lit up. 'He'd help. I know he would. We'll show him from the Tree-house. He wouldn't let the case be buried then, would he?'

He hugged his duvet-wrapped knees happily, then said, 'Too bad about the Moonlight Treasure Hunt, though. It would have been great.'

Primrose closed her eyes and thought of her waterfall of gold coins shining in the ghostly light of the moon. She sighed. It was indeed a great pity.

At half past twelve, they waited for Mr Tom by the front gate. He came whistling down the road, breaking into a smile when he saw them.

'What a pair of earnest faces!'

'Mr Tom. Mr Tom. We want to talk to you.' Bobby and Primrose tried to speak at the same time.

He looked surprised, but leaned on the front pillar and said, 'Fire away.'

They told him about the Treasure Chest.

'Please, Mr Tom, please, *please* open it for us,' Bobby begged.

Mr Tom rubbed the side of his nose with a finger, thinking. At last he appeared to come to a decision. Signalling for Primrose and Bobby to follow, he walked around to the back door, opened it and stuck his head into the kitchen.

'Be along in a moment, Emerald. Just going down to the Tree-house with this pair.'

He shut the door again and said, 'Right. Away we go.'

Primrose and Bobby ran on ahead of him, to open the window of the Tree-house and set up the telescope. They had everything ready by the time Mr Tom came puffing up the ladder.

He peered through the telescope at the suitcase, saying, 'Likely there's nothing much in it.'

117

'But there is!' protested Primrose. 'We heard it rattle.'

'Nothing of value, I mean.' Mr Tom straightened up and surveyed them with his lips pursed. Then he said, 'Oh well, I suppose we'll have to take a look, anyway — can't have you two dying of curiosity for the rest of your lives.'

'Oh, thank you, Mr Tom!' They threw their arms around him in delight.

'Right, then. I'll tell you what to do. Straight after dinner, skedaddle, and let me talk to Pandy.'

Pandy! If he talked to Pandy, that would be the end of it. But, feeling they'd pushed their luck enough with Mr Tom, Bobby and Primrose said nothing and tried not to let their disappointment show on their faces.

As soon as was decently possible after dinner, Bobby and Primrose excused themselves and went out into the garden to wait.

Everything hung in the balance now, and it was out of their hands. Bobby hopped from foot to foot with impatience, while Primrose sat on the front pillar, watching the house.

Eventually Mr Tom came out.

'Hop to it,' he said quietly as he approached them, 'before Pandy changes his mind.'

They didn't need to be told twice. Off up the road they ran, with Mr Tom following behind.

When they reached the County Council offices, Mr Tom went inside for a few minutes. He came back out with

Mr Boggle, who was carrying a long brown jute sack, like the ones Mr Popplehanger had used for clothes. Mr Boggle held the sack up in front of Primrose and Bobby.

'This big enough? Or will we need the wheelbarrow?' And he laughed, a deep, uproarious belly-laugh that made his whole body shake.

'Don't tease the kids, Barney,' said Mr Tom.

Mr Boggle stuck the sack under his arm, still laughing, and the four of them set off for the Treasure Chest — up the road towards the public dump, then around to the left in the direction of the Scrabblemongers' house. The area was quiet, as work had stopped for lunch.

They went around to the ramp and climbed down into the moat. It was now half-filled with rubble. There was only a narrow strip of the moat bottom left uncovered, below the fence, and they walked along this until they were opposite the Treasure Chest. In front of them, the pile of dumped rubble rose halfway up the Sandwich Mountain.

'Climb carefully, now,' said Mr Tom. 'We don't want any broken ankles.'

The rubble was indeed dangerous, with many gaps where a foot or even a whole leg might slip down. However, with Mr Tom leading and Mr Boggle bringing up the rear, Primrose and Bobby climbed until they were standing safely on a large slab of concrete below the Treasure Chest. It was just out of reach.

But not out of Mr Tom's reach. He banged on the suitcase with a clenched fist, and it rattled.

'See! See!' cried Bobby, nearly falling off the slab with excitement. 'We told you.'

'Do that again, Mr Tom,' begged Primrose, trying to decipher the sound.

Mr Tom obliged. The rattle was definitely made by metal things — small metal things, like coins, shifting around. Primrose's insides felt fluttery; the sensation was almost unbearable.

Mr Tom looked at the case, then at the rubble beneath them, and took off his jacket. He laid it on the slab below the Treasure Chest.

Mr Boggle wasn't looking at the case at all. He was leaning against the Sandwich Mountain, watching their faces, a wide grin on his own.

It's just a huge joke to him, thought Bobby furiously, and suddenly he didn't like Mr Boggle much any more.

Primrose hadn't taken her eyes from the case; she was afraid of missing the first glimpse of their treasure.

Mr Tom produced a large penknife. Carefully he stuck the blade into the top left-hand corner of the case and sawed downwards, then across, then upwards, forming a flap. He pulled out the knife and inserted it into the bottom of the flap, forcing it outwards until he could get his fingers in as well. He pulled hard.

Instantly, a waterfall of shiny silver and gold and bronze and flashing colours poured down the face of the Great Sandwich Mountain, onto the jacket beneath.

Primrose and Bobby stared in amazement.

'There's more yet,' Mr Tom was saying, as he put his arm deep inside the Treasure Chest and swept out pile after jingly pile, sending it all cascading down to form a mountain of its own at their feet. Mr Boggle was laughing, his belly heaving up and down and his big shoulders shaking.

Bobby and Primrose looked at their treasure.

Coins, bottle-tops, badges, medals, buttons, beads, caught the sunlight in a medley of glistening colours. Bobby and Primrose dived for the coins together and picked up one each. Bobby examined his. It had the words 'UNITED STATES OF AMERICA' and 'FIVE CENTS' stamped on it.

He peered at Primrose's coin. Hers was smaller — so small they could hardly make out the print.

'UNITED ... STATES ... OF ... AMERICA,' Primrose read. 'ONE ... DIME.'

She looked hopefully at Mr Tom, who shook his head and said, 'I don't think it's worth much, pet.'

'Nickels and dimes,' sang Mr Boggle, 'nickels and dimes!'

They checked some more of the coins, but none of them were any different from the ones they had. Bobby bent down and picked up one of the medals. It had a crest on the front, and when he turned it over he saw an inscription on the back: '3rd Place, Three-Legged Race.'

He dropped it back into the pile.

Primrose was running her fingers gently over the top of the heap. She picked up a giant mother-of-pearl button, with soft iridescent colours, and a dark-red bead that gleamed like a ruby in the palm of her hand.

'Well, it's treasure all right,' said Mr Tom. 'Magpie treasure. You've got a fair few coins there, all the same.'

Mr Boggle was still laughing as Mr Tom asked him to hold the sack open. They heaped the treasure in, handful by handful.

The sack was very heavy when it was filled, so Mr Tom and Mr Boggle took turns carrying it over their shoulders as they all made their way back to the County Council offices. The mess-room was full — most of the workers from the dump were there, just finishing up their lunches. The contents of the sack were displayed for everyone to see.

Mr Boggle announced that, strictly speaking, he was entitled to a reward. So he swiped a handful of treasure, which he put into a jam-jar. He danced around the mess-room with the jar clutched to his chest, laughing uproariously.

Bobby tried to scowl; but, in spite of himself, he felt the corners of his mouth twitching. So when Primrose burst out laughing, he did too. Mr Tom joined in, nodding approval.

Soon everyone was laughing and joking and teasing, making such a racket that Mr Charlie Checker, who wasn't on his lunch hour, left his hut and came over to see what was going on. So Bobby and Primrose told him — about the strange, exciting, but above all totally *ridiculous* treasure they had found.

They laughed themselves silly.

Then it was back-to-work time for the drivers of the lorries and bulldozers and compactors and excavators. One by one they departed, in a high good humour, and Mr Tom took Primrose and Bobby home.

In the Scrabblemongers' kitchen, the treasure was emptied into Starlight's old baby bath, to be duly admired by Pandy and Emerald. It was very quickly removed to the table-top when Starlight decided that treasure was for eating. Emerald told them that a dime was worth ten cents, and confirmed what Mr Boggle had said — that a five-cent coin was called a nickel.

Later on, Bobby and Primrose set to work picking out all the nickels and dimes. It took them two days. When the coins had been counted into piles, the grand total came to $76.10. It was quite a lot of money.

Then Emerald had to explain to them, gently, that no bank would exchange foreign coins as small as these. The only place they could spend the money would be America.

'We'll keep the money for you, then,' said Primrose, 'for when you go on your travels.' And Bobby, though bitterly disappointed, thought that was the best idea too.

Then Primrose and Bobby began to worry that, maybe, the treasure wasn't really theirs. But Mr John sent word that, this time, it was finders keepers, and he promised to keep his ears open for anybody going on holiday to America who might be willing to exchange the money for them. So perhaps sometime, they thought, they'd get to spend the treasure after all.

And Emerald said she could think of plenty of uses for the rest of the treasure, too.

●

Within a week, the moat was gone.

A neat layer of soil covered the ground on all sides, extending for a considerable distance all around. It was perfectly levelled, right up to the bottom of the Scrabble-mongers' garden fence, without even a mark to show where the moat had been.

The machinery was gone. Primrose and Bobby could see it on the skyline, working far off in the direction of the gully.

The Treasure Chest was gone, too.

And the Great Sandwich Mountain was gone, buried with all its secrets for ever and ever....

– 21 –

Changes

Back at school, in September, everyone was talking about the exciting news.

The place where the dump had been was to be turned into an adventure park, with a lake, hills and forests, swings and roundabouts and slides. There would be a proper assault course; it would have rope bridges, high ladders above the lake, and huge nets for climbing.

It was like a dream come true.

Suddenly Bobby and Primrose had more friends than they could cope with. They became the two most popular children in their school.

That Christmas, they got a very strange letter from Great-Aunt Holly, and a big parcel addressed to both of them. It contained a book about basic mountaineering, and another book about Mount Everest, with photographs so magnificent you nearly felt you were there.

'I know I shouldn't be encouraging you,' Great-Aunt Holly finished her letter, 'but if either of you ever gets to climb Mount Everest when you grow up, keep an eye out for my sweetheart's body. He was wearing a red anorak and had a silver locket with my picture in it around his neck.'

'Is it really true — all that?' Primrose asked Emerald. But Emerald only smiled, and bagged the books so she could read them first.

●

Every day now, Primrose and Bobby watched from the Tree-house as work progressed on the new park.

The machines were back again, with loads and loads of rubble and soil, which were heaped in some places to make hills. Then the hills and the flat bits alike were covered with layers and layers of soil. Trees were planted, and grass. A huge lake was constructed, covering the place where the pits had been, and the area around it was landscaped so that it looked as if it had been there for years and years.

Pipes were delivered, to make tunnels big enough to cycle through and smaller ones to crawl through. Huge piles of logs and poles went to make the assault course, and the picnic tables and benches, and the lookout towers. There were hobby-horses and swingboats, too, and enormous slides set into the sides of hills. When it was finished, there wasn't a finer adventure park in the whole country.

All this took a very long time, of course, but eventually the park was ready.

Pandy was appointed caretaker, as he lived so near the job. Emerald got the position of chief grass-cutter, driving the big Council tractor with its mowing-blades behind. And, best of all, Primrose and Bobby and Starlight (who was now quite a young lady) had free entry to the park any time they liked.

But sometimes, Bobby and Primrose would look out through the window of their Tree-house at the beautiful park, with its trees and shrubs and flowers, its brightly painted swings and slides, and feel only a sense of loss. For somehow it didn't seem half as exciting as their old desolate landscape of wire fences and flying rubbish, bulldozers, lorries and skips; or their moat, with its Great Sandwich Mountain, Scary Scary Monster, and real Buried Treasure.

It wasn't anything as magical at all.

ALSO BY MARGOT BOSONNET

THE RED BELLY TRILOGY

Up the Red Belly

Once you dive into the woods, you're hidden from the adult world.
So many secret places! Best of all is up the Red Belly, the giant tree
with a splodge of red paint on its trunk.

Mackey's just moved to the suburbs. He's a streetwise boy who
thinks he's cool — but with the new kid comes trouble. And poor
Felicity always seems to get blamed....

'I give it top marks, ten out of ten.'
Books Ireland

ISBN: 0-86327-530-3

Red Belly, Yellow Belly

For the Red Belly Gang, the trouble starts when Harold decides to
set up a rival gang and call their tree the Yellow Belly.

And that's not all! What's lying in wait at the haunted gate-house?
Will Mackey and Dara ever learn to get on? And why, oh why, are
Felicity's parents making the gang spend their summer tidying up
mad old Fitzy's garden?

'A pleasure for old fans, and a maker of new ones.'
Children's Books Ireland

ISBN: 0-86327-640-7

Beyond the Red Belly

The Red Belly Gang's summer is heading for disaster — property
developers have plans for Conker Woods! The gang want to save the
woods and — most of all — the Red Belly tree itself.

The battle is on! Protests, sit-ins and even an alliance with the Yellow
Belly Gang help their cause. But is it all enough to save the Red Belly?

ISBN: 0-86327-755-1

WOLFHOUND PRESS, 68 Mountjoy Square, Dublin 1, Tel: (01) 874 0354